Newfound

A Richard Jackson Book

Newfound

A Novel by
➤➤➤ ⫷⫷⫷

Jim Wayne Miller

ORCHARD BOOKS
A division of Franklin Watts, Inc.
New York

Orchard Books
A division of Franklin Watts, Inc.
387 Park Avenue South
New York, NY 10016

Manufactured in the United States of America
Book design by Jeanne Abboud

10 9 8 7 6 5 4 3 2 1

The text of this book is set in 11 pt. Janson.

Library of Congress Cataloging-in-Publication Data

Miller, Jim Wayne.
Newfound / Jim Wayne Miller.
p.   cm.
"A Richard Jackson book."
Summary: A boy growing up in his grandparents' house in the
Appalachians learns about the town and the people around him, their
habits, stories, and lore.
ISBN 0-531-05845-X.—ISBN 0-531-08445-0 (lib. bdg.)
[1. Appalachian Region—Fiction.]   I. Title.
PZ7.M6184Ne   1989
[Fic]—dc19   89-42540
                                                   CIP
                                                   AC

FOR MY NEWFOUND FAMILY,
FRIENDS, AND NEIGHBORS

"Each of us is all the sums he has not counted. . . ."
—Thomas Wolfe
Look Homeward, Angel

Newfound

⇶ I ⇷

THE LAST DAY of school fell on a Tuesday, and we were back home by midday. My little brother Eugene and my sister Jeanette scrambled down off the yellow school bus in front of me and started running up from the big road toward our house. Feeling old and wise—for I had just finished fifth grade—I walked slowly, thinking about the whole summer that lay before me like the high green pasture on the mountain back of our house.

Although they had run on ahead, Eugene and Jeanette soon slowed to a walk. Then they stood waiting, looking first toward our house, then at me, as if they weren't sure whether they should go on in.

"Look, Robert!" Jeanette said, as I caught up with them. She pointed to Dad's old Studebaker parked under the big sycamores. "Daddy's home early, too." Jeanette sounded as if she didn't know whether to be glad he was home or not.

Now, that's strange, I thought. Why would Dad be home from work so early?

Eugene and Jeanette hung back now and followed me

inside the house. There sat Dad, all reared back in his chair, his eyes bright and black as chinquapins. Mom's eyes looked like dark thunderclouds. We all wanted to know why Dad was home so early from the mines.

Mom said, "Because he got fired, that's why!"

Dad said, "Riley Ford *thinks* he fired me. I quit."

Mom was all torn up, but Dad was calm. He kidded us children and tried to make us laugh. "These young'uns have just started their summer vacation," he said. "I just may vacate with them—all summer!"

Mom said having us home all summer was all she could stand, let alone having him underfoot, too.

"I'll stay out of your way," Dad said. "I'll swing me a hammock out there between the sycamores."

Mom said she hated to cash in the two fifty-dollar bonds, but she guessed she'd have to if Dad didn't find work, for we didn't have a red cent laid back.

Dad told her not to fret, he was just kidding about laying off all summer. He said he was going to start work tomorrow morning.

"You've already got another job?" I asked. I hoped so, for when Dad quit a job, it made Mom nervous and afraid, and the house felt strange.

"Where?" Jeanette said.

"What kind of job?" Eugene asked.

Dad wouldn't say anything except that he was going into business for himself.

Uh-oh, I thought.

"James Wells!" Mom said. "You've been in business for yourself before. Looks like that should have been enough to cure you!"

THE NEXT DAY a truck came groaning up from the big road. Dad helped the driver off-load a hundred bags of cement, a big cast-iron contraption that stood on four legs, and about two hundred short wooden boards.

When the truck had gone, Mom came out of the house and stood looking at the stacked bags of cement, the wooden boards, and the upright iron machine. She kept her distance, as if it all might explode.

Dad motioned to the machine. "You know what that is?" he asked Mom.

"I don't know what it *is*," Mom said, "but I know what it's *not*—it's not a living."

"You just might be surprised," Dad said.

Mom made Eugene, Jeanette, and me come away from the machine. I was trying to figure out how it worked. "What does it do?" I asked Dad.

Dad explained that it was a machine for making cement blocks. The wooden boards were pallets.

Jeanette thought it must have cost at least a hundred dollars.

"Didn't cost me anything," Dad said. Frank Cornett had been owing and owing him, and Dad figured he never was going to get the money, so he took the block-making machine instead.

The way Dad explained it, he'd got a good deal, but I could see Mom was mad as a hornet.

Dad cocked his head and looked at her. "Do you have any notion what one of these things costs?"

Mom took Jeanette by the hand, turned, and without saying a word led her back to the house.

Eugene and I stayed outside and helped Dad. We put about half the sacks of cement in the garage, along with the block machine. The rest we restacked neatly beside the garage and covered with a tarpaulin. Dad could carry a sack of cement easily. I could have carried a sack by myself, too, but Dad said Eugene and I should carry a sack together.

Mom and Jeanette came out of the house and stood watching us work. Well, Mom sighed, at least we had the two fifty-dollar bonds, and we could cash them in if Dad didn't find work.

"Woman, I've found work! Don't you understand?" Dad said. He rolled his eyes at Eugene and Jeanette and me, and tried to make a joke out of the whole thing. But Mom didn't think it was a bit funny—especially when Dad added that he'd already cashed in the two bonds, to buy the cement.

I thought Mom was going to cry.

"It takes money to make money," Dad said. "Capital. You invest, you get a return on your investment. That's business. The whole dad-blamed country operates that way."

Mom said it sounded like gambling to her.

"It *is* gambling," Dad said.

⇶ ⇷

DAD HITCHED UP the old two-wheel trailer to the Studebaker, and that afternoon Eugene and I helped him haul sand up from the big sandbar at the creek. Eugene got tired, and Dad said he could just play in the creek, so he did.

Dad and I kept on hauling sand. The Studebaker would hang up in reverse and Dad would be a long time, rocking it back and forth, getting it to go forward. He hammered together a mixing trough and toward evening we were all set up.

Dad called for Eugene to come on up from the creek, where he'd been playing. He called Mom and Jeanette out of the house to show them how the machine worked. We stood watching as he mixed up a small batch of cement. He shoveled the mixture into the machine on a wooden pallet, tamped it tight, twisted some screws on the side, tightened the top down, and finally removed a cement block with three holes in the center, smooth sides, and ends hollowed to half-circles.

It was neat! I ran my hand along the smooth, cool side of the block and looked up at Mom. I wanted her to like it.

Dad did, too. "Look at that!" he said to Mom. "Ha, ha! Just like making biscuits!"

He explained to Mom how the blocks had to sit out in the air on the wooden pallets, be sprayed with a hose, and allowed to harden. He could sell the blocks for fifty cents each, probably, and he figured when he really got the hang of it he could make maybe two hundred a day.

That would be a hundred dollars a day! I thought. How could Mom argue with that? I grinned at Dad, then looked at Mom to see what she would say.

But who would he sell them to? Mom wanted to know.

I looked back to Dad, who seemed irritated.

"To anybody who wants to buy them!" he snapped.

Mom said we'd been living here all this time and there hadn't been any call for cement blocks.

"Nobody's ever made any, either!" Dad said. He told me

Mom never had understood business and he doubted if she ever would.

We went into the house for supper.

Dad's right, I thought, as we sat eating. If somebody on Newfound Creek had made blocks before now, people would have bought them. Dad was right about it, surely. Anyway, I thought the block machine was neat, and I wanted to help him make blocks and learn to work the machine myself. I wanted us to make hundreds of blocks, thousands!

⇒⇒ 2 ⇐⇐

THE NEXT DAY we flew to making blocks. Dad employed me to heap up sand at sandbars along the creek. He didn't say how much he'd pay me, and I never asked. At first he hauled the sand on the trailer, pulling it with the Studebaker. And he let me steer. But the old car locked once and for all in reverse, and Dad almost broke his neck trying to back the trailer all the way to the house. The rest of the day he tinkered with the car, trying to use parts from the other old cars down in the field below the house (the ones Mom's chickens laid eggs in, the ones Jeanette, Eugene, and I played in), but none of the parts would work.

Just when Dad had given up trying to fix the Studebaker, Mom came out and stood looking at all the greasy gears on the ground. She said, had it occurred to Dad that he might be able to use some parts from the old cars down in the field below the house. Dad just sat looking up at her with grease on his forehead where he'd wiped away sweat with the back of his hand.

Well, Mom wanted to know, couldn't he use some of the parts from the other cars?

No, Dad said. They wouldn't work.

Mom said she was just trying to help, she didn't see why they wouldn't work. Then she turned and went back into the house.

Dad and I walked over to Grandpa Smith's to borrow his white mule, Bertie, and a sled. Grandma and Grandpa Smith, Mom's parents, and Grandma and Grandpa Wells, Dad's parents, all lived on the same big farm, within walking distance of where we lived. It was Grandpa Wells's farm, but Grandma and Grandpa Smith lived there, too, in an old gray house up the creek above Grandma and Grandpa Wells's house, which was white and not as old.

Walking along the road with Dad, I got to thinking about how all my grandparents lived on the same farm, and I told Dad I didn't know any other kids whose grandparents all lived so close, the way mine did.

He said he didn't, either.

Their living there that way had always seemed natural to me, but as I thought about it, while we walked, it began to seem strange.

"Grandma and Grandpa Smith work for Grandpa Wells, don't they?" I asked Dad.

Yes, but still they did pretty much as they pleased, Dad said.

"Does Grandpa Wells pay Grandpa Smith?" I asked.

"No," Dad said. "Your Grandpa Smith makes a crop and splits the money from it with your Grandpa Wells."

"Why?" I wanted to know. Maybe because Dad had quit his job again and was going into business for himself, I wanted to know more about the different ways people made money. "Why do they split the money?"

"Because it's Grandpa Wells's land," Dad said.

"Have Grandma and Grandpa Smith always worked for Grandpa Wells?"

"Not always," Dad said, "but for a long time." He picked up a rock and sailed it at a fencepost.

I knew it must have been a long time, because Mom had told me she lived there with her parents when she was a little girl.

Grandpa Wells had a store, too, the Trading Post, that Grady Plemmons ran for him. We bought our groceries there. Grandpa Wells didn't work, exactly. He used to work, but a long time ago he'd got his left hand cut off in a silage cutter. Now he looked out after things, and had several people who worked for him. He wore khaki trousers and suit coats and a stockinglike sleeve on the stump where his left hand had been. Sometimes he wore a khaki stocking on his left arm, sometimes a blue one. He owned the house we lived in.

"Why don't we just borrow Grandpa Wells's truck to haul the sand?" I asked Dad.

We could, Dad said, but he'd rather not. Not just now.

We walked right past Grandma and Grandpa Wells's big white house and on up the creek to Grandpa Smith's. Going through the woodlot, we scared Grandma Smith's guinea hens, making them screech and go *potterick, potterick*, which caused Grandpa Smith's foxhounds in their shaded lot in the pines to start barking. Grandma Smith came onto the porch to see what was the matter, and Grandpa Smith stepped out of the barn. We said it was just us, and we wanted to borrow Bertie. Grandpa Smith called the white mule from the pasture with a nubbin of corn.

After that I hauled sand up from the creek on a box sled with Grandpa Smith's mule. I'd go after Bertie in the morning, and Grandpa Smith would harness her up for me. I knew how to do it, but I wasn't tall enough yet to throw the harness across her back. Bertie wore a big straw hat with holes cut for her ears. Grandpa Smith would set the straw hat on Bertie's head and hand the lines over to me. I hauled sand, geeing and hawing and working the bit in Bertie's frothy jaws. After a few trips from the creek to the garage, Bertie knew exactly how to go, and I could let the lines go slack.

I had some time to play, but mostly Dad and I made blocks. No air stirred in the garage, and Dad worked with his shirt soaked through, humming "Where There Will Be No Setting Sun." We carried the blocks out into the sun and left them on their wooden pallets. In the evening we sprayed them with a hose, and the first thing next morning, after they had hardened, we restacked them and freed the pallets for that day's run. It turned out that we couldn't make but about a hundred blocks a day, and some days, when a piece on the machine broke—the same piece kept breaking again and again, and we had to take it to Lloyd Sluder's blacksmith shop—we couldn't get a hundred made, sometimes not even fifty.

But even a hundred blocks a day—that was fifty dollars, Dad told Mom.

"Where's the money?" Mom said. She said she needed to buy some more jars and lids to can blackberries, and to make blackberry jelly and jam.

June was as good as over and Dad hadn't sold the first block.

Mom threw it up to him that now we had no car, and she couldn't go where the best blackberries were. The ones by the house, where she'd been picking with Jeanette and Eugene, weren't very good. But on Cook's Mountain, where her brother Clinton lived, the briers were thick and the berries as big as your thumb. We'd always gone to Uncle Clinton's toward the end of June to pick blackberries. But now we wouldn't get to, Mom said, and we'd have very little jelly and jam come winter, and very few canned berries for pies. And if Dad thought the store bill we'd already run up was something, she went on, then wait and see what it would be come winter. Peaches. That was another thing. She always bought peaches from the peddlers who came around. But there'd be no money this time, so we'd have no peaches, either. And Dad had fiddle-faddled around in the spring, when Ed Reeves had had three litters of pigs—three litters —and we hadn't bought one, and so come fall we'd have no hog to slaughter, no ham, no shoulder meat, no sausage.

"Will you ever wind down?" Dad said, wild-eyed. He buttered a piece of hot cornbread and looked around the table at us children.

Everything Mom said was true. While she talked, I'd be on her side. But when Dad looked over at us and gave me a knowing look, then I was on his side. I wanted him to sell some blocks and prove to Mom he could make money with the block machine.

Mom said she wouldn't wind down. She reminded Dad that we were eating new potatoes and green beans and tomatoes and peas and squash and okra from Grandma and

Grandpa Smith's garden. Grandpa Smith came every day with a basket of this, a bucket of that. And other things we needed we were buying out of Grandpa Wells's store—on credit. Mom threw that up to him. It was the farmer who was secure, she said. The farmer always had work, and food to put on the table.

"I have work!" Dad said.

"Um—hummm!" Mom said disdainfully. She recollected aloud that years ago Grandpa Wells had tried to get Dad to take over the job of running the farm, but, no, Dad had to traipse off to the mines, drive a truck, then try to go into business for himself, then go back to driving a truck for the mines. If we had stayed on the farm, we'd be well off now. It broke her heart, Mom said, after all these years, still to be living off her mama and papa—and his.

Dad said he hadn't been cut out for a farmer, and Mom had never understood that, either. Oh, he loved the smoked ham and garden greens, he admitted, but that didn't make him a farmer.

And it was true: green growing things seemed to wither at his touch. Once Mom had kept after him until he ordered some seedling trees to set along the edge of the yard. Not one lived. Finally, Mom herself went back on the ridge above the house and pulled up some little white pines by the roots and set them out along the edge of the yard. Now they were as pretty as Christmas trees.

No, Dad could stand oil and grease and coal dust, but he couldn't stand fresh-plowed dirt in his shoe-tops. I'd seen him plow a row or two of corn at Grandpa Wells's, and once or twice he'd helped out at tobacco-setting time. He never lasted long, though, and he looked little and lost standing in plowed ground.

─❯❯❯ ❮❮❮─

THE FOURTH OF JULY came and went. Dad and I made blocks. The stack of blocks grew so high Mom wouldn't let Jeanette and Eugene go near it for fear a block might fall on them. Dad started another big stack out a ways from the first one. People passing on the road in cars and trucks would slow down to see what was going on. Neighbors stopped in the evening, when the stacks cast long shadows, and stood around and talked and just looked at the blocks. Gooberneck Surrett ran his car off into the ditch below the house; everyone reckoned he was looking at the blocks and paying no attention to where he was driving.

Finally, the loafers who hung around Grandpa Wells's store in the evening started coming up to our house instead and standing around looking at the blocks and talking. "Don't let that crowd start hanging around here," Mom told Dad. She didn't say anything to me and Eugene, but she made Jeanette stay in the house.

Dad never tried to keep the store crowd from coming to our house. He didn't say anything when they hustled up some boards, laid them over blocks, and made benches to sit on. They even pulled up the horseshoe stobs down at the store, brought them up to our house, and pitched horseshoes till dark, and then sat in the dark, talking and smoking. Kennie Murphy and Marvin King got into a fight one evening; Kennie accused Marvin of pushing his horseshoe back from the stob in the measuring, and cheating him out of a leaner. Wiley Woods was always circulating, trying to get up a poker game. But nobody bought any blocks.

⇶ 3 ⇚

MOM WAS GRIM NOW. She put it to Dad all the time about letting loafers hang around, drinking, fighting and gambling, running off the road in front of the house. The days came on like blocks laid end to end, and Mom kept putting it to Dad. Here we were into August, she said, but Dad kept fiddling away, as if he thought the summer would never end, and still he hadn't sold block one. And it wouldn't be long before we children would be starting back to school, and there wasn't a red cent to buy school clothes. And look at us: holes in our pants, no shoes at all, and there wasn't even money to buy mill-end goods that were on sale every day in Jewell Hill —material she could make us shirts from, and dresses for Jeanette.

Riley Ford came from the mine one day at suppertime and asked Dad to come back to work, said they needed him.

Dad said he wasn't interested, being in business for himself now.

I thought Mom would explode. "A man comes after you," she said, "practically begs you to come to work! But no!" Her eyes misted up. She said she'd had about all she could stand. She was thinking of just taking us children and leaving—moving in with Grandma and Grandpa Smith. That was all she knew to do.

Mom's words ran through me like an electric shock. "No, Mom," I said, shaking my head.

Eugene started to cry.

Jeanette put her fork down. Her chin trembled.

Once before, when Dad had gone into the restaurant business (it was a beer joint! Mom said), she'd taken us and moved first to her sister Frances's, then back to Grandma and Grandpa Smith's. I remembered it as the worst time in our lives. Dad would come on Sunday and he and Mom would talk, and then argue, and Dad would stomp off the porch and roar away in the car. I moped about. The old gray house was creepy. Eugene had not been walking long (Jeanette was just a baby), and he'd wander into the dark room and the fur collar on Grandma Smith's coat would scare him and he'd drop to his hands and knees and come rumbling out of there, big-eyed, muttering "Comin' on, comin' on!"

We had always liked to drive to both grandparents' houses on Sundays. We'd stop at Grandma and Grandpa Wells's first and visit a little while, then go on up to Grandma and Grandpa Smith's, where we stayed longer. Mom didn't like to stay long at Grandma and Grandpa Wells's. But if Dad wasn't going to be around, we didn't want to go back to Grandma and Grandpa Smith's to live. The time we stayed there had been so strange; I remembered how the ground had seemed unsteady under my feet. No.

Mom sulked at the table. Dad talked to us, but hardly a word passed between him and Mom now. She'd take a bite and look out the window, and tears would well up in her eyes, and she'd leave the table and go into the front room. Dad teased us and tried to cheer us, but our faces were long. Even though words were flying through my mind like whole flocks of birds, my throat ached, and I could barely answer Dad above a whisper.

Finally, even Dad grew glum.

➜》》 《《←

THE BLOCK MACHINE broke again—in the same place. When we carried the piece down to Lloyd Sluder, he turned it over in his hands and shook his head. He'd fix it, but he'd already fixed it so many times, he doubted it would hold. And sure enough, it broke again after Dad had made about ten blocks. Well, Dad said, there wasn't but about a sack and a half of cement left, anyhow.

Tiptoeing around the house, Eugene and I heard Mom and Dad talking. "Money!" Dad said. "You don't want money, you want what money buys."

"I have neither the one nor the other," Mom said.

Dad came out of the house, the screen door slammed, and he went walking off down toward Grandpa Wells's store, his hands in his pockets. We children sat out under the sycamores in the front yard, our heads down, fearing what might be going through Mom's head. Oh, we hoped she wouldn't take us and go to Grandma and Grandpa Smith's!

"I won't go!" Eugene said, punching the ground with a

stike. "I'll run away before I'll go." He packed some things in a shoebox and vowed he was ready to strike out.

Dad was back from the store around suppertime. Without a word, he reached into his shirt pocket, took out our store bill, and laid it on the table in front of Mom. It was marked across the front: PAID. I saw Dad could hardly keep from breaking into a big grin.

Grandpa Wells had just marked the bill PAID, Mom said.

Not so, Dad said. He'd paid the store bill.

Where in the world did he get the money? Mom wanted to know.

He didn't get any money, he said. He just let Grandpa Wells have enough blocks to build a shed over his grease pit in return for that store bill marked PAID. There were more ways than one to skin a cat, Dad said.

That proved it, Mom said. Grandpa Wells had just marked the bill PAID, but Dad hadn't really paid him anything.

"I paid him blocks," Dad insisted. Grandpa Wells wouldn't have made the deal if he hadn't been satisfied, Dad said.

The next day Coy Marler, who lived on Grandpa Wells's farm, too, like Grandpa Smith, came in one of Grandpa Wells's trucks and hauled three loads of blocks down to Grandpa Wells's store. Dad was off and gone. We didn't see much of him the rest of the week. He'd eat and strike out. An hour or two later he might appear in a truck with somebody, and they'd load on blocks, or he might be gone until after dark and come walking in.

But whether Dad was home or not, for the next three or four days there was a constant coming and going at our house, so much traffic Mom was afraid we children might get run over. Motors roared, gears groaned, men hollered, directing the trucks to back up. Tailgates dropped, chains rattled across truckbeds. Men were out there at the blocks working until nine and ten o'clock at night, laughing and talking. They loaded blocks onto one truck, working by the light of another truck's headlights. They even pitched horseshoes out there by shining headlights onto the horseshoe pits.

When all the coming and going commenced, the stacks of blocks looked like black mountains against the night sky, but soon they began to dwindle.

It appeared that Dad had gone all over the place putting notions into folks' heads. He said, "Some people don't always know what they need; you have to show them." And what deals he made! He traded a bunch of blocks to Essie Carver, the widow, for the awfullest bunch of jams and jellies and peach preserves. We had to get cardboard boxes from the store and go bring it all home. Dad had sold her on the notion of having a little pump house built to keep her pump from freezing in winter. Essie had all those preserves, she put them up every year, like a squirrel putting up hickory nuts, she said, always more than she needed. In fact, she didn't much care for sweets; it was Mr. Carver who had always liked her preserves and jams.

Dad traded blocks to Ed Reeves for a three-quarters-grown Poland China pig. Ed brought the pig in his truck and helped Dad herd it into our pen that had been standing empty since last Thanksgiving. Ed aimed to use the blocks he hauled away for a bridge abutment. He'd been driving through the creek for years, and probably would have kept on doing it, he said, if Dad hadn't come around horse-trading.

"Now you've played hob," Mom said. "Us with nothing to feed that hog."

Dad winked at me. "You wanted a hog, by golly. Now you've got one." He said the trouble was, Mom thought he was as simple as she was. He pulled some weeds and threw them in to the pig. We fed it scraps and more weeds that evening and the next morning. Then Morris Prestwood came with a truckload of last year's corn, still unshucked. He made a couple of trips back for blocks. Morris allowed he'd underpin his house with them.

I went with Dad down to Hill Hargis's. Hill admitted he'd like to build on to his house. Everybody knew Hill made good money bootlegging, but he swore he didn't have the money to add on to his house. Dad traded him blocks for half-gallon jars of whiskey. At first Mom thought it was more canned goods. Dad opened a jar and let her smell. She backed away as if she thought the Devil himself would leap out, like a genie.

Dad sold six gallons at one shot to Claude Ball, who was shell-shocked and drew a government check. Dad knew to catch Claude just when he'd drawn his check. The rest of the whiskey he sold by the jar to men who came around in the evening to load blocks or to pitch horseshoes.

Now Dad had a roll of money. He teased Mom with it. He'd hold it out to her, and when she'd reach for it, he'd draw it back.

"I aim to have that money!" Mom said.

But Dad was too quick for her. "You don't want it," he said. "You want what money buys."

Finally, he let her take the money away from him. She put it down in the front of her dress. Dad vowed he'd get it back, but Mom crossed her arms over the money, and though he tickled her, she never uncrossed her arms.

But they were laughing again, and that was the best thing. We children felt like playing—for the first time in more than a week.

→⫸ ⫷←

SOMEWHERE IN HIS DEALINGS Dad got hold of a bicycle. It was on the front porch one morning when I got up. He said it was mine—for the work I'd done all summer. Oh, it was the best secondhand bicycle in the world! "That'll have to be your Santy Claus, too," he said.

Riding the school bus that fall, when I started sixth grade, we could see Dad's blocks everywhere. There was the new shed over the grease pit at Grandpa Wells's store, Essie Carver's new little pump house, Ed Reeves's bridge across the creek, and ever so many houses underpinned, the blocks painted over. And here and there you could see blocks stacked up, waiting to be put to some use.

Dad got rid of every block. People stopped coming to the house in the evening. The loafers moved the horseshoe pits back down to the store. Dad got a red Chevrolet pickup, and the Studebaker took its place alongside the other old cars in the field below the house and became a hen's nest. Dad went back to work in the mines. "But only temporarily," he gave Riley Ford to understand.

One evening he took a bunch of things out of the pickup and showed them to us. There was a mask, a thing with a pistol grip, and a metal tank.

"James Wells!" Mom said. "What on earth?"

"It's a welding outfit," Dad explained. He aimed to turn the garage into a welding shop.

"I'll declare to my soul," Mom said. "How much did you have to pay for that?"

"Nothing," Dad said. "Buck Boyd—he's been owin' me and owin' me."

DAD HAD BEEN RIGHT when he told Riley Ford he'd come back to work only temporarily. He got his eye hurt working with the welding outfit and quit driving a coal truck for Riley Ford. He wore a patch over his left eye, grew a mustache, and lay on the bed playing solitaire and reading. He traded the Chevrolet pickup for a two-door Ford.

A week or two after he hurt his eye, he started leaving the house in the afternoon, about the time Jeanette, Eugene, and I would be coming home from school. We'd see him standing before the mirror, shaving, trimming his mustache. He'd leave the house wearing slacks and a sport shirt, looking brash and adventuresome, his face hard and freshly shaven, the patch over his eye. The last time he had dressed up and left the house in the afternoon was when he'd gone into the restaurant business with somebody named Pete Ramsey in Mountain City. Mom always said, anytime it was mentioned, that it was not a restaurant, it was a beer joint and pool hall—and worse. I wondered what she meant by worse.

One morning I heard him and Mom arguing in their room, and it sounded like the same argument they'd had when he'd gone into the restaurant business before. Mom was crying. "I can't stand it, I tell you. I can't live this way."

A drawer slammed hard. "You never had it so good," Dad said.

"But I can't live, not and enjoy it, not when I know how it's got."

"You can't live and enjoy anything, no matter how it's got. You never had anything, you've lived at the head of a holler so long, and been to so many prayer meetings with some old goat of a preacher bending over you, looking down at—"

"Hush," Mom said. "Just hush."

He went out the back door, still pulling on his shirt, got in the Ford, and drove off. Three days later he still hadn't come home.

Even when he'd been gone four days, I still had hopes of his coming home, until the afternoon I returned from Grandpa Wells's store with a bag of groceries Mom had sent me after—and saw that Mom had packed suitcases. There they stood in the living room, along with a cardboard box tied with string, and two full shopping bags.

I didn't look at Mom as I passed through into the kitchen. I set the groceries on the table and leaned against the sink, letting the water run cold in a glass, feeling my heart beating in my fingertips.

I could see Eugene out in the backyard playing on his sand mountain. Jeanette was in her room. I checked. She was coloring in her coloring book.

In the living room Mom started humming. She was sitting barefoot by the window combing her hair. She had long black hair that reached down to her waist when she stood, for she'd never cut it. It was a sin, I'd heard her say, for a woman to cut her hair, which was her glory. She hummed and combed. Then she stopped humming and combing at the same time and just sat, her hands folded in her lap.

"How can we go anywhere?" I asked.

She said she could send word to her brother, Uncle Clinton.

"But—if we'd wait—"

She stood. She was twisting her hair, knotting it, piling it high on either side of her head, in a way that made her look old.

I went into the bedroom I shared with Eugene and lay down. A fly buzzed in the far corner. The screen door slammed when Eugene came in from his sand mountain. He ran the faucet. The pipes knocked. I could hear him prowling in the groceries I'd brought home, and I expected to hear my mother scold him, but she didn't. For a long time I heard only the stirrings caused by the heat in the walls and ceiling. Then my mother started humming again.

When I woke it was dark. I knew I must be at Uncle Clint's, for I remembered going over the swinging bridge to his house there at the foot of Cook's Mountain. But I couldn't remember Uncle Clint's coming for us. I had to go to the window and look out to convince myself I had been dreaming, that I was still at home. Squinting, I stepped into the living room, where the suitcases stood, then went to the kitchen. Jeanette was sitting at the table. She looked up at me over the rim of a glass of milk. When she set the glass down, I said, "You have a milk mustache."

The bedroom door opened. I turned and saw Mom coming out—and Dad came out right behind her! He had come home! I just stood there looking at them, while Dad came sidling up to me, pulled my head against his chest, rubbed it hard with his knuckles, and asked me how I was.

We had a late supper. Dad told jokes and watched to see how heartily we laughed. Mom got hiccups. "Don't move!" Dad said suddenly, staring at the floor by her bare feet. "There—a mouse by your toe!" Mom jumped, almost upsetting the table. When she realized he had tricked her, trying to frighten her to make the hiccups go away, she sat down again. Dad looked at her, she looked at him, and Jeanette and Eugene and I laughed when she hiccuped again. Mom laughed too. Right in the middle of her laughing she gave another little jump and we laughed even harder. Suddenly I realized I was not laughing, but crying, or laughing and crying at the same time. I tried to stop shaking and couldn't.

After supper we sat in the living room, acting as if we did not see the suitcases in the corner. Dad stood by the mantelpiece and put a lot of change into the big thick-glass piggy bank that belonged to Eugene, Jeanette, and me. He had rolls of quarters. He had been putting change into the bank for as long as I could remember, and it was so heavy I had to hold it with both hands.

He brought a cedar box out of the bedroom, and Mom and Jeanette and Eugene and I sat watching him as he went through all the interesting things in it. He showed us some Confederate bills, and I passed them on to Eugene, who wanted to hold them. He showed us some old coins he emptied from a leather pouch. Among the coins was a small gold medal. Dad said he had won it in a speaking contest at school. Eugene liked the medal, but he didn't know what a speaking contest was. Dad stood up and started speaking; he made gestures, pointing first at me, then at Eugene, speaking the speech that won him the contest. It was about self-reliance. Eugene and Mom looked embarrassed.

"I still remember it, by golly—most of it," Dad said.

"You always did know how to talk," Mom said.

Dad winked at me. "How do you think I ever got your mama to come down out of that holler over home and marry me?"

"How?" Eugene said. "How?"

"I talked her into it, that's how." He grabbed Mom, set her on his knee, and bounced her up and down.

"Yes," Mom said, struggling to get free. "That's what they should have given you the medal for."

5

WHEN I AWOKE the next morning, I ran to the door, looked out, and saw that the suitcases were gone. So was Dad—to work, Mom reckoned. But the way she said it left doubt.

It turned out he had gone back to work for Riley Ford at the mine. But he wasn't driving a truck, he was doing electrical work. At home he shut himself off in the bedroom, listened to the radio, and studied books on electricity. Once I saw him reading my dictionary. At Grandma Wells's on one of our Sunday afternoon visits, I happened to mention that Dad read the dictionary. Grandma Wells looked thoughtful and said Dad had never realized his potential. I could tell Mom didn't like that; she gave a little smirk. I thought about what Grandma Wells had said. I wanted Dad to realize his potential, but I also wanted him at home with us, and no suitcases in the hall.

March had come in like a lion. I was doing fractions at the kitchen table when the radio stopped playing in Mom and Dad's room, the door flew open, banging against the wall, and Dad stepped out with his cedar box. "Who's been in this?" he wanted to know.

Mom, who was sewing a dress for Jeanette, answered almost in a whisper. She didn't know.

Dad cursed and threw the box in the corner, breaking the lid off. "Somebody's been in it and I want to know who!"

Mom tried to act as if his throwing the box had not bothered her, but I saw her eyes were wild. "I said—I don't know."

"Have you been in that box, Robert?" he asked me.

"No, I have not."

"Jeanette?"

"No."

"Eugene, have you?"

Sitting on the sofa beside Mom, Eugene snuggled against her. He dug his feet into the rose-colored cushion and put his head under Mom's arm.

Dad jerked Eugene to his feet. "Have you been in the box, Eugene?"

Eugene's lips moved, but no words came. He swallowed, then nodded.

"Stop scarin' him," Mom said.

Dad looked at her. The muscles in his jaw flexed. "Somebody took my coins and my medal."

"I think I did see him playin' with some of that old money," Mom said.

"You think—? Well, why in hell didn't you take it away from him? Why?" He cursed again. He shook Eugene until Eugene's teeth clicked.

"I don't care what he done with it," Mom said. "It's not worth anything, anyhow."

Dad turned Eugene loose, picked up the pieces of the cedar box, and set them on the mantel, beside the bank. He stood looking at Eugene, glaring, breathing hard. Eugene had backed up to Mom again. She pulled him close.

"What did you do with the things in the box, Eugene?" Dad asked.

Eugene looked up at Mom. Rings in his sweaty neck held thin black lines of dirt.

"You better answer me, buster!" Dad grabbed Eugene, tearing him away from Mom, jerking him to the middle of the room. Eugene's teeth clicked together again, and his shiny black hair fluffed up and down as Dad shook him. "Answer me!"

"In the y-y-yard," Eugene got out.

Dad turned him loose, then reached for him once more.

"Don't lay another hand on him," Mom said. "Don't!"

"Hush, before you get in trouble, too," he said.

He went past her into the kitchen, got the flashlight, and went out the kitchen door. Eugene did not begin to cry until Mom did. She was on her knees, on the floor, smoothing his hair. "Now look what you've done," she sobbed.

I went out into the backyard where Dad was searching with the flashlight—in the grass, and on Eugene's sand mountain—for the lost coins and the medal. I found three coins in the sand. Each time I handed one to Dad, he held it in the light, turned it over in his hand, then threw it into the darkness. We never found the medal. Telling me to go back into the house, he got into his car, turned fast, and went bouncing down the gravel drive.

We went to bed. I was awake a long time after Eugene, in the bed beside me, had stopped sobbing. I was still awake when Dad returned. I heard the car door slam, the kitchen door opening, then his footsteps in the living room, then glass breaking in the kitchen. Eugene sat up suddenly just as I left the bedroom. Mom had already come out of her room and was in front of me. When I saw Dad, he was holding a hammer and for a second I thought he was going to kill Mom. Then I saw the glass pig on the table, smashed to pieces. The money, spilled out on the table, melted and ran together.

Dad raked coins off the edge of the table into a cigar box. "I'll pay you back, bud," he said to me.

"I don't want it!" I shouted. "I don't! I don't care!"

Mom turned in front of me and went into the living room, taking Eugene, who had come up behind us, with her. Jeanette followed in her long nightgown. "I've had all I can stand, James Wells," Mom said. "I just wish you'd go on and not come back."

He kept on raking coins into the cigar box.

"I mean it. I don't aim to be here if you come back. You hear me?"

"I hear you."

A minute later he went out the back door with the cigar box.

I stopped crying. I didn't realize I'd been crying.

From our back bedroom, where Eugene was sleeping again (I didn't think he had ever really been awake), I watched day break. Mom had been moving about in the hall since Dad left, and when she called me, I stepped out and saw the awful suitcases standing there again.

6

M OM SENT WORD TO Uncle Clint, and he came
for us in his old Plymouth, but we didn't go to
his house at the foot of Cook's Mountain. Mom
had him take us right over to Grandma and Grandpa
Smith's. If we hadn't had the suitcases, boxes, and shopping
bags, we could have walked. Except for missing Dad, I
didn't feel I'd left home, for I had always gone back and
forth between our house and Grandma and Grandpa
Smith's. Bertie, Grandpa's mule; Sarah, the brindled milk
cow, and Betsy, the black-and-white one; his foxhounds,
Luke and Leader, Jamup and Honey; the chickens that
walked poles to roost in the trees at night; the snake-headed
guinea hens that screeched and pottericked when they were
excited—all this was familiar to me. And Grandma Smith
made us apple turnovers, let me drink coffee, and treated
me more like I was grown-up than Mom did.

Eugene kept his promise and ran away, but I figured I
knew where he was. Grandpa Smith and I went to the little
pole house Eugene and I had built once, up on the ridge in

the pines, and, sure enough, there sat Eugene, with his shoebox of belongings—his sack of marbles, some comic books, a pair of socks, and some jelly biscuits. Grandpa Smith didn't scold Eugene; he just told him he'd better come on home before the bears started stirring in the pine woods. Eugene cocked his head and looked up at Grandpa Smith as if he hadn't thought of that. He gathered his things and came on back to the house with us.

When Grandma Wells found out Mom had brought us back to Grandma and Grandpa Smith's, she sent Mom word: Mom was to bring the children back down to Grandma and Grandpa Wells's and live there—where we would have "a better environment," her note said. (Mom folded the note and laid it on the mantelpiece, beside the big clock, and I read it later when she was out in the barn gathering eggs with Grandma Smith.)

"When I lived down there before, I said if I ever got away, I'd never be fool enough to go back, and I won't," Mom said to me. She told about how she and Dad had lived upstairs at Grandma and Grandpa Wells's right after they were married, and until I was about a year old. Dad was gone from the house every day, working. Mom said Grandma Wells ordered her around and snapped at her, and gave her to understand she didn't know anything.

"I wasn't but seventeen," Mom recollected, "and there was a lot I didn't know. But she was just mean. I'll never forgive her."

I sat by the stove in the kitchen and listened as Mom talked and cooked supper. Jeanette had gone with Grandma Smith to milk, and Eugene was helping Grandpa Smith feed his foxhounds. Mom stood over the stove and told something else Grandma Wells did to her. She said that when I was a baby I was colicky, and cried a lot, and Grandma Wells would call upstairs for her to make me stop crying. When Mom couldn't get me to stop, Grandma Wells would stand at the foot of the stairs and say how it grieved her that her James had married an ignorant field hand, and if she'd had it in her power, it would never have happened. I would keep on crying and Grandma Wells would threaten to come upstairs and take me away from her and send Mom packing back up the holler, where she belonged.

"Now, Mr. Wells wasn't like that," Mom said, "but he was like James, off and gone most of the time, and he never heard it. And when I'd tell James, he either wouldn't say anything, or he'd act like he didn't believe me. I endured it about a year before, finally, I talked to Mr. Wells, and he let us move out of there and into our own house. He'd just bought it from Roy Redmon. If it'd been up to James, we'd never have left. He never would have. But I couldn't stand it another minute. Why, I felt like I was in jail there. I'll never forgive her for the way she treated me. . . . Thinks she's so fine. Never forgive her. I know you're supposed to forgive, but I can't."

I was hearing all this for the first time, and I was almost twelve. It helped me understand why Mom never liked to go to Grandma and Grandpa Wells's and, when she did go, why we never stayed long, and why Grandma Wells and Mom hardly ever said a word to one another while we were there. Listening to Mom, I remembered Grandma Wells saying how lazy people were, and how you couldn't get anybody to do anything, and if you did, they couldn't do it right. I could turn somersaults on the living room floor up at Grandma and Grandpa Smith's, but I felt like I had to sit up straight in the living room at Grandma Wells's, where it was always cool and quiet. But Grandpa Wells was different—Mom was right about that—not saying much except to look up from a book of *The History of the World* and joke about something.

During the first few days after we moved to Grandma and Grandpa Smith's, Mom kept remembering things Grandma Wells had done to her. We were walking the creek bank looking for cresses. A cold wind blew. The sun kept breaking out of the clouds, then disappearing again. Mom remembered something else. "When I was no more than four or five years old," Mom said, "she accused me of something and caused me to get a whipping."

She told how Grandpa Smith was building a new set of porch steps down at Wellses', and she was there with him, just a little girl, playing around in the yard where he was working. She played with the carpenter's level and had fun making the bubble in the level stand between the lines, or she would tilt it first to one side, then the other. Two or three times Grandma Wells came around where the steps were being built and told Grandpa Smith to take the level away from that child—meaning Mom. And then in the afternoon, when the steps were finished and Grandpa Smith couldn't find the level, Grandma Wells reminded him that Mom had been playing with it and had probably carried it off somewhere. Grandma Wells made a big fuss about the level, for it belonged to Grandpa Wells, not Grandpa Smith. Grandpa Wells had said it didn't matter, but Grandma Wells kept on about it. After they'd looked everywhere and couldn't find it, Grandpa Smith had given Mom a good whipping—switched her legs and ankles with a keen willow switch. "I never carried that level off," Mom said, "but she

caused me to get a whipping over it, and I've never forgot."
A long time later, when we were washing the cresses we
had gathered, Mom was still thinking about what she'd told
me. "I don't know to this day what happened to that level,"
she said.

⟫ 7 ⟪

GRANDPA SMITH SAID spring was as late coming as he'd ever seen it, but the weather turned warmer as the days lengthened. One evening in early April it was finally warm enough to sit out on the porch after supper. Peepers called from the creek and willows along the bank had turned the faintest green. A car with its parking lights on drove up the road, turned onto the wagon road, and came toward us. I thought I knew the sound of the car, and when it came closer, I saw it was Grandpa Wells's big green Hudson Hornet. He stopped at the edge of the yard, and Jeanette and Eugene and I ran over. Grandpa Wells didn't offer to get out of the car. He just sat behind the wheel and let the car idle. He smiled at us and called us young sprouts. Grandma Wells leaned across and asked me to tell Mom to come to the car. I ran back to the yard and told Mom.

"She might just as well have stayed at home," Mom said. "Anyway, if she wants to talk to me, she can come to me. I'm not at her beck and call."

"Now, Nora," Grandma Smith said. She was patching one of Grandpa Smith's shirts.

"I'm not," Mom repeated. She said to me: "Tell 'em to get out and come over."

I ran back to the idling car and told Grandma and Grandpa Wells what Mom said.

It was getting dark, but I could see Grandma Wells's lips stick out and then quickly become very thin. "Tell your mother we didn't come to visit, and I would appreciate it if I could have a word with her."

I ran back to tell Mom what Grandma Wells said.

"I'll talk to her but it won't do her any good," Mom said, and she got up from her split-bottom chair and walked out to the car.

She made me stay in the yard, and sent Jeanette and Eugene back from the car, too. We couldn't hear what they said, even when Grandpa Wells cut off the motor. A minute later he cut it on again, and we thought he was leaving. Then he cut it off again before he finally started up and pulled away slowly.

"What was that about?" Grandpa Smith asked.

"Just what I said. Why, I'd sooner hold my hand to the eye of a hot stove than move down there."

Grandpa Smith sat a minute looking toward the road, then chuckled, as if at a joke no one else had heard. Then he got up and went into the house.

⇒≫ ≪⇐

GRANDMA WELLS NEVER CAME to talk to Mom again, and she didn't send any more notes. But when Jeanette, Eugene, and I were down at her house, she would look up at the ceiling and ask, "What's going to become of you children?" And sometimes, when we'd be telling something that happened at Grandma and Grandpa Smith's, she'd mumble things. "What kind of environment! . . . Growing up like weeds!"

We had moved to Grandpa and Grandma Smith's in early March of that year. I was more than halfway through the sixth grade. Just as we had before Mom brought us back there, we caught the yellow school bus weekday mornings. I would sit on the school bus and look at J. D. Marler and his little brother Carl and Mack Woody, whose families also lived on Grandpa Wells's farm. I'd think about their fathers, Coy Marler and Jess Woody, and about their mothers and brothers and sisters and grandparents. I looked at houses as we rode along, and imagined living there with Mom and Dad and Eugene and Jeanette. I'd have imaginary arguments with Dad in which I talked him into coming back home.

After school I'd walk back down to our old house and sit on the hill looking at it, standing empty. Eugene and Jeanette missed our house, too. Sometimes we'd start out walking together, knowing where we were going but not admitting it to each other. We'd end up sitting together on the hill and looking at our house with the sycamore trees and the garage where Dad had made the blocks last summer. Eugene and I would hold blades of grass between our thumbs and blow on them. We made sounds like Grandma Smith's guineas screeching, or else sad sounds, like someone crying. Jeanette said she bet Dad would come and take us back to our house; he'd come back once before. Eugene said Mom wouldn't go back, even if he asked her to. Hadn't

Jeanette heard Mom say that a hundred times? I knew Eugene was right, but I wanted Jeanette to be.

Living with Grandma and Grandpa Smith wasn't as good as being at home, but not nearly as bad as I had imagined it would be when Mom first threatened to take us and leave. Still, I would wake in the night sometimes and think I was at home in our old house, and I would lie a long time before I realized, all over again, that I was at Grandma and Grandpa Smith's.

Mom said we weren't going to live off Grandma and Grandpa Smith, we'd pull our weight. She got a job at Blue Ridge Manufacturing, the clothing factory in Jewell Hill, and rode with Carlene Cantrell, who worked there, too, and lived further up the Newfound Creek road. Dad got a job as a long-haul trucker, driving a big eighteen-wheeler down into Alabama or Georgia, or out to Arizona, New Mexico, and California. He drove with another man, and they took turns sleeping, because there was a bed right in the truck, up behind the driver's seat. The first time he came to see us after he started driving, he brought me a T-shirt with a New Mexico desert scene painted on it. He brought Eugene a model eighteen-wheeler, and Jeanette a Georgia belle doll.

Dad was also partners with the same man he drove trucks with in a miniature golf course and driving range in Mountain City. Then he had a put-and-take trout pond over on Spring Creek at the same time that he managed a nightclub back in Mountain City.

One Saturday morning in May Carlene Cantrell came by in her old blue Chevrolet to take Mom to Mountain City. While Carlene waited outside in the car, Mom sat us down and explained that Dad was going to meet her in Mountain City and they were going to see a lawyer and get a separation. I felt my chest heave at the sound of the word. Eugene sat picking at the corner of a cushion on Grandma and Grandpa Smith's old brown sofa. Jeanette bit her lip. Then she looked at Eugene and said it was Eugene's fault, because he had lost Dad's coins.

Eugene wiggled down on the sofa, his chin on his chest, the way he'd done when Dad had asked him about the coins.

Mom shook a finger at Jeanette and said, "Don't ever let me hear you say that again! Don't you even think it!" She said Eugene wasn't to blame for anything. The problem was that she and Dad had different notions about how people ought to live—always had thought differently. For a long time she had thought Dad would change, and she supposed he had thought she would change. Finally, she had realized Dad wouldn't ever change, and she knew she wasn't going to. So they were separating, and after they had been separated a certain length of time, they'd get a divorce. It was all their doing—Mom's and Dad's—and Eugene had nothing to do with it. Did Jeanette understand that?

Jeanette nodded.

Mom brushed Eugene's hair out of his eyes. He sat up straight on the sofa.

Usually, if Mom went to Mountain City without us, we asked her to bring us something, but this time we just waved hesitantly as she left with Carlene. We didn't ask her to bring us anything, and we were quiet all morning.

I thought about what Mom had said—how it wasn't Eugene's fault that she and Dad were separating. I knew she was right. For as long as I could remember—and I could remember longer than Eugene or Jeanette—Mom and Dad had disagreed about where he ought to work. When he went into the restaurant business, they'd argued, and Mom had brought us back to Grandma and Grandpa Smith's. Eugene hadn't had anything to do with that.

Even after we'd moved to Grandma and Grandpa Smith's this second time, I think we still hoped we'd eventually go back to our own house. In Jeanette's doll-town, which she had built in the pines above Grandpa Smith's dog lot, she'd made pinecone dolls of us still living in our own stick house—and Dad was there with us. But after Mom went to Mountain City to meet with Dad in a lawyer's office, I began to lose hope. And more and more I was coming to understand that Mom was right about how different she and Dad were. I think Jeanette stopped believing we'd go back home. I never heard her blame Eugene again for Mom and Dad's differences. One day when I walked through the pines above Grandpa Smith's dog lot, I saw that Jeanette had changed her doll-town: our stick house was empty, and the pinecone dolls that represented Jeanette, Eugene, Mom, and me were in the big stick house with the pinecone Grandma and Grandpa Smith. Beyond a pile of pine needles Jeanette had raked together to make a mountain, her Dad-doll sat in a new stick house she had built for him.

Still my hope of our going back home held on, like honeysuckle that clung all winter to fenceposts at the corner of the pasture by the barn, and now grew greener and higher.

⤜ 8 ⤛

M OM HADN'T BEEN working long at Blue Ridge
Manufacturing in Jewell Hill before she started
acting strange, the way Dad used to. After supper she'd go in the back bedroom, where she and Jeanette
slept, and close the door and be quiet for a long time.
Sometimes she'd come out with a lot of crossed-out numbers
on a page in a notebook and ask me if I could help her work
a problem. Once she said she knew a pile of wood contained
twelve cords, and that it was four feet wide and eight feet
high, but she needed to know how long it would be. We
figured it out. Another time she came out saying a man
wanted to put a fence around a lot. The distance was five
hundred feet. The fencing cost him $7.95 per hundred feet,
plus the cost of fenceposts twenty feet apart at $.55 per
post. She couldn't get her figures to come out the same as
the answer in the back of her book. I worked on the problem
and couldn't get it to come out right, either. We told the
problem to Grandpa Smith. He drew lines on a sheet of

paper to represent the posts set twenty feet apart and figured out that you needed an extra post at the end, so you needed twenty-six posts instead of twenty-five, which was the figure Mom and I had been using.

Mom needed to know how many miles fifteen kilometers were. She had to convert centigrade to Fahrenheit, and vice versa. She borrowed my math book, because she understood it better. She looked in Grandma's almanac and the big *Book of Knowledge*. She talked to me about John Quincy Adams, Aphrodite and the Cyclops, the Norman Conquest and the Battle of Waterloo. She looked up rivers and mountains on maps in my books. She wanted to know where "water, water everywhere" came from, and I knew, because we had read "The Rime of the Ancient Mariner" in school.

At supper one evening Mom informed us that there were a million seconds in twelve days, but it would take thirty-two years to make a *billion* seconds. As for a *trillion* seconds, that would be about thirty-two thousand years.

What was going on?

When Carlene Cantrell came by to pick Mom up weekday mornings, she would sometimes come in and have a cup of coffee before they left for Blue Ridge Manufacturing. Carlene was a short, red-haired woman with a round face, and she was always laughing. One morning, when they were drinking coffee and I was getting ready to go to school, I heard Carlene say, "Lord, Nora, if I could do it, I *know* you can! You stick with it, now, you hear? Don't you give up."

Give up what? Was Mom about to lose her job or thinking about quitting? I didn't hear what Mom had said, so I didn't know what Carlene was talking about, but I agreed with her. I didn't want Mom to give up, or even think about it.

One evening when Eugene, Jeanette, and I were doing homework, Mom came out of the back bedroom with a problem about angles and degrees. She didn't know why one angle was 90 degrees and another was 45 or 120. I showed her with a protractor. "It's like a pie," I said. "A whole pie is 360 degrees. If you cut it in two equal pieces, each piece has 180 degrees."

Mom nodded.

"If you cut the two pieces into two pieces, they'd each have 90 degrees."

"But what if it's not a pie?" Mom said.

"Makes no difference. It could be anything."

"Mom, can I have some pie?" Jeanette said.

"No."

Grandma Smith was making a rag rug. "I think you ate all the pie, anyway."

"Did you?" Eugene said. "You'd better not have."

"You all are getting me off the subject," Mom said, and went back into her room.

→≫ ≪←

IT SEEMED AS IF Grandma and Grandpa Smith were the parents and Mom was a kid again, doing her lessons with me and Eugene and Jeanette. One evening she came out with a problem in compound interest. She wasn't sure whether she had it right or not. She didn't. Eugene looked at it but said they hadn't studied interest in his grade yet. Mom and I worked on the problem together, and she went back into the bedroom.

Grandpa Smith was mending a piece of Bertie's harness with an awl and some leather thongs. He gave me and Eugene and Jeanette a problem. If he started out giving us each a penny and doubled it every day for a month, how much money would we have? We set to work.

"Wow!" Eugene said.

I looked on his paper. He was up to the sixteenth day.

"We'd be rich, that's what!" Jeanette said. "How much would it really be, Grandpa?"

"I've forgot. I've not figured it lately."

"Will you do it?" Jeanette asked. "Will you give us a penny and double it every day?"

"I couldn't do that. Nobody could."

My pencil flew as I raced to keep ahead of Eugene. Still we finished at about the same time. "One billion, seventy-three million, seven hundred forty-one thousand—"

"—Eight hundred and twenty-three pennies," Eugene finished.

"Sounds about right," Grandpa said.

"How many dollars?" Jeanette wanted to know. She had given up.

"Divide by a hundred," Grandpa Smith said.

Eugene figured. "It's going to be over ten million," he said.

"What month did you give us the pennies in?" I asked. "Thirty days hath September, April, June, and November. If you gave the pennies in some other month, like in October, they'd double again on the thirty-first! Then it would be over twenty million dollars."

"I better give you them pennies in February," Grandpa Smith said. "Save me a lot of money."

ONE EVENING WHEN MOM CAME OUT and looked in *The Book of Knowledge* and went back into the bedroom, Jeanette said, "Mom's going to school, just like us."

"How do you know?" I said. We were alone. Eugene was out in the smokehouse with Grandma and Grandpa Smith.

"Because after she makes me go to bed, she stays up and does lessons. She has this big notebook in her bag."

When Jeanette was getting a snack out of the pie safe in the kitchen, I went back to Mom's room and knocked gently on the door. Her chair scooted back. She came to the door and opened it a little. "Mom, are you going to school?" I asked.

She stood, still holding the door partway shut. "Well, sort of." Then she opened the door and let me step inside. She said she was studying for her high-school diploma through a program offered at Blue Ridge Manufacturing. It would help her to get a better job there. She'd wanted to keep it a secret until she finished—if she ever finished.

"You'll finish, Mom," I said.

"Maybe by the time you do," she said.

→≫ ≪←

I LOOKED IN her book called *Subjects for Home Study* one day when she was still at work and saw where all the arithmetic problems and the questions about history and literature were coming from. Mom had a marker at a section on the family. There were sections called Marriage in Modern Life, Divorce, The Larger Family Group, and The Modern

Family. The section on divorce said children were usually hurt by the divorce of parents, but it might be even worse for children to be raised in a situation where the parents were unhappy. Mom had underlined that—and also parts of The Larger Family Group that said uncles, aunts, grandparents, cousins, even remote ancestors, were all part of the family.

➤➤➤ 9 ⬅⬅⬅

I N LATE MAY, when the tobacco plants were about six inches high, we helped Grandpa Smith pull them from the big plant bed and set them out in the field. The bed was about ten feet wide and a hundred feet long and covered with cheesecloth to protect the plants against late frost. Once when we went to the plant bed, we discovered that a rabbit had got under the cheesecloth. It jumped around, making the cheesecloth rise like a little tent wherever it went. Eugene and I tried to catch the rabbit, but it got away and went bounding off into the woods.

Grandma Smith and Eugene dropped tobacco plants in the rows, about a foot apart, and I came along behind, making a little hole in the ground with a wooden stick Grandpa Smith had whittled for me. I stood the plant in the hole, filled the hole with dirt, and pressed the dirt down so the plant would stand up straight. I got so I could do it all in one quick motion. Jeanette came behind me with a pail of water and a tin cup and watered each plant. Grandpa

Smith had made her a little pond in the creek beside the field, where she could fill her pail with water.

I FINISHED THE REST of the sixth grade in early June. Eugene finished fourth, Jeanette second. With school out, I helped Grandma Smith hoe in the big garden, and as we worked, I'd tell her about things I'd read or heard on the radio, and I'd ask her all sorts of questions. When we chopped weeds from the rows of potatoes, we stood opposite one another in the rows, Grandma Smith in her wide-brimmed straw hat, hacking away, pulling the loose soil up around each plant. Sometimes, working like that, we'd both strike at the same spot with our hoes and get them tangled at the hoes' goosenecks. The first time that happened, Grandma Smith said, "That's a sign. When two people get their hoes tangled, it's a sign they'll be working in the same place come another year."

"Why is it a sign?" I asked.

"It just is. I've always heard it."

I wanted her to explain everything. When I was younger, I never questioned why things were as they were. Until that day the summer before when I was walking along the road with Dad, going to get the mule, Bertie, and the sled, I hadn't thought there was anything special about all my grandparents living on the same farm, one grandfather working for the other. Then the situation began to seem unusual to me, even odd. And since Mom and Dad had separated, I wanted to examine everything; I wanted to know how families were put together, and why things were as they were. Grandma Smith said I could ask more questions than seven wise men could answer.

Still, she knew all sorts of things. She could conjure warts; she said something over a wart on Eugene's hand and made it go away. Jeanette got too close to the cookstove and burned her arm, and Grandma Smith knew how to draw the fire from the burned spot. She waved her hand and said:

> *"There come an angel from the east*
> *Bringing frost and fire.*
> *In frost, out fire!*
> *In the name of the Father, Son, and Holy Ghost."*

Then she put some salve on Jeanette's arm and Jeanette stopped crying. Grandma Smith knew spells to make butter come, and when she had Eugene and me take turns working the dasher up and down in the wooden churn, she taught us rhymes to say that would make the flecks of butter appear in the buttermilk.

She knew things about honeybees. Grandpa Smith had five beehives—he called them "bee gums"—and one day when we were working in the garden and Grandpa Smith was off helping Coy Marler, Grandma Smith dropped her hoe and ran toward the house as fast as she could. I looked in the direction she had looked, and saw that a great dark cloud of bees was rising from one of the bee gums. Grandma Smith came back out of the house with a pie pan and a big spoon, and she ran along under the slowly moving cloud of bees, beating the pie pan with the spoon. She followed them far down into the pasture below the garden, still beating the pie pan, where the swarm settled on the limb of a jack pine. The bees were so heavy they made the limb droop toward the ground, like a branch weighted down with snow in winter. Then she sent me to find Grandpa. When he came he brought another bee gum from the barn, cut the whole limb off the tree with his pocket knife, and carried the swarm of bees to the new gum. Reaching into the clump of bees with his bare hand, he found the queen, coaxed her into the new gum, and finally the whole swarm followed her into their new home.

When it was all over, Grandpa Smith grinned and said, "If your grandma hadn't made them bees settle, they'd a been gone to the mountain, and even if I ever could have found them, I would have had to cut them out of some holler tree."

I went to the woods with Grandma Smith to hunt for guinea nests. (Guineas were bad about stealing their nests away, she said.) On hot afternoons we'd stand by fence rows and cow trails listening for half-wild guineas screeching after they laid eggs in nests they'd hidden in thickets, briers, scrub pines, and chinquapins. And when we'd find a nest, Grandma Smith wouldn't take the eggs from it with her bare hand; she carried her little garden hoe, and she'd reach into the nest with the hoe and carefully roll the eggs out, one at a time, always leaving one, so the guinea would continue to lay eggs there. Because I went with her, I knew where all the hidden nests were, and she would sometimes send me alone to gather the guinea eggs.

But she always warned me to watch out for snakes. There were "spread natters" in the cut-over woods where the guineas concealed their nests, she said. I looked but never saw one. Did she mean "spreading adders"? I wondered. Grandpa Smith told stories about snakes. Once a rattlesnake bit his ax handle, he said, and the ax handle swelled up into a log so big they hauled it to the sawmill, sawed it up, and made enough lumber to build a house. But when the house was painted, paint thinner made the swelling go down. The house shrank until it was no bigger than one of Jeanette's dollhouses! You had to watch out for rattlers and copperheads, he said. They were the poisonous snakes where we lived. But blacksnakes were all right. Grandpa Smith let a big blacksnake live in the barn because it caught mice. I saw it sometimes lying between the logs.

While we were out gathering guinea eggs one afternoon, Grandma Smith told me a story about her great-aunt, who was stabbed by her husband a long time ago. Someone had written a song about the tragic event, and Grandma Smith could sing it:

> *"Come listen, friends, while I relate*
> *Of a crime committed in Tennessee state.*
> *It was the murder of poor Lottie Yates.*
> *I hope she's passed through heaven's gates."*

That reminded her of another old song that must have come from across the waters, Grandma Smith said. It was about a girl named Little Margaret. She sang:

> *"Little Margaret was sittin' in her high-balled home*
> *Combin' on her long yellow hair.*
> *She saw sweet William and his new-made bride*
> *Comin' down the road so near."*

Little Margaret was angry because William had married someone else, and she threw down her ivory comb. That night, all dressed in white, she appeared at the foot of William's bed and asked him how he liked his pillow, his sheet, and the fair young girl fast asleep in his arms. Then she disappeared. William got up and rode quickly to Little Margaret's house, where he found Little Margaret in her coffin. Grandma Smith ended the song:

> *"Once he kissed her lily-white hand,*
> *Twice he kissed her cheek.*
> *Three times he kissed her cold, cold lips,*
> *And fell in her arms asleep."*

I thought about the story. "If William liked Little Margaret, why did he marry the other girl?" I asked.

Grandma Smith didn't know.

"Was Little Margaret already dead when she came to the foot of the bed and talked to William? Was she a ghost then?"

Grandma Smith thought so. She had heard tell that the spirits of people would appear to their loved ones, even nowadays.

"Has anybody's ghost ever appeared to you like that?"

"Well, no." But Grandma Smith said she had dreamed about people, had such horrible dreams that she woke up worried about them, and come to find out, something bad had happened to them.

Thinking about Lottie Yates, who was killed and had a song written about her, I remembered the night Dad came back to the house and broke the glass piggy bank with a hammer, and how I'd thought at first he was about to hit Mom. I went over and over the story of Little Margaret and William and imagined Mom appearing, all dressed in white, at the foot of Dad's bed in Mountain City. I pictured him getting out of bed and driving to Newfound Creek. . . . And what about Aunt Vi, Dad's older sister, who was a teacher in a college in Pennsylvania, and who had never married? Had she ever had a tragic love affair?

One day when Eugene and Jeanette and I were down at Grandma and Grandpa Wells's, we found some old shoeboxes that mud daubers had built on, down among straw and tobacco sticks out in the big barn—shoeboxes tied up with red and blue ribbon. The boxes had Aunt Vi's name on them. We untied the ribbons and found lots of letters, all to Aunt Vi. Some were from soldiers, and some had S.W.A.K. written on them. When I told Jeanette S.W.A.K. meant "sealed with a kiss," she giggled.

We tied the ribbons around the boxes and put them back under the straw and tobacco sticks. And when Aunt Vi came home from Pennsylvania for a few days in July, Eugene, Jeanette, and I made a special trip down to Grandma and Grandpa Wells's just to see her. We stood in the parlor where she sat drinking coffee and talking with Grandma and Grandpa Wells. We studied her gray-green eyes, the freckles on the back of her hand. I saw she had some white spots under her fingernails, and later I told Eugene and Jeanette I knew what the white spots meant.

"What?" Eugene asked.

"There's a white spot for every sweetheart you've had. Grandma Smith told me. And I bet Aunt Vi has a white spot under her fingernails for every sweetheart who wrote her all those letters we found."

Jeanette looked at her fingernails. She said phooey, she had some white spots under her fingernails, and she sure didn't have any sweethearts.

I explained that the white spots meant either how many sweethearts you have had, if you're old, or they could mean how many you were going to have, if you were a kid like Jeanette. "Let me see how many," I said.

But Jeanette made tight fists and ran away and wouldn't let me see.

⋙ 10 ⋘

THAT SUMMER WE HAD tender new potatoes from the patch we'd planted, and okra and cucumbers, onions, peppers, and tomatoes from the garden. When we went with Grandma Smith to pick sweet corn, Jeanette said, "Mind your tongue in the cornfield, because there are lots of ears listening! Right, Grandma?" Grandma Smith said that was right.

She made rhubarb pies for us. On weekends she and Mom canned corn and beans and tomatoes and little pint jars of chopped pickles called chow-chow. "What's green when they're red, and ripe only when they're black?" Grandma Smith asked. "Blackberries, of course!" Jeanette said. Grandma Smith said the blackberries were ripe, and she sent us out on the ridges and into the pasture fields to pick them. She and Mom made blackberry jam and jelly.

In July peddlers came by with a truckload of peaches. Grandma and Mom bought several bushels and canned them. Eugene and Jeanette and I washed mason jars all summer, it seemed. After the jars came out of the pressure cooker, and before we carried them to the cool can house, they stood on shelves in the kitchen overnight. Before I went to sleep, I'd sometimes hear a jar lid go *plink*. The lids made that sound when they sealed, Mom said.

One Saturday afternoon Grandpa Smith robbed his bees. He stood over the bee gums wearing gloves, a long-sleeved shirt, and a wire cage over his head. He puffed smoke from his bee smoker on the bees to stun them and frighten them away. Eugene ate some of the honey while it was still warm, although Grandma Smith warned him not to, and the honey made him sick. I got too close to the gums and an angry bee buzzed my head, got tangled in my hair, and when I tried to slap it away, it stung me right on top of my head.

Mom, Jeanette, and Grandma Smith stayed in the house with the doors closed until Grandpa had finished taking the racks of honey from the gums. Then they cut the golden honey out of the racks and stored it in jars. Grandma Smith said she probably should have come outside and allowed herself to get stung on the hand, because a bee sting was good for arthritis. The jars of honey were a smoky blond color next to the yellow peaches on shelves in the can house. We had honey with buttered biscuits for breakfast, and that August Mom and Jeanette used some honey in a birthday cake for Grandma Smith.

Dad left word at Grandma Wells's that he was coming on Saturday instead of Sunday. Grandma and Grandpa Wells had a telephone. He planned to come early and take us to Mountain City.

"Why does he want to take you all the way over there?" Mom said.

I remembered Mom and Dad arguing about whether to go to Jewell Hill or to Mountain City. Mom liked Jewell Hill, where people came in from the country to sell their cattle and corn and tobacco, and bought things at the little department store or the hardware. Dad always wanted to go to Mountain City, where he was living now. It was farther away, and bigger, with lots of traffic lights, and tourists. Mom called them summer people, but Dad said more and more the summer people were living in and around Mountain City all year. It was a coming town, Dad always said, whereas Jewell Hill—except for Blue Ridge Manufacturing—was so small and sleepy you might as well put the Welcome and Come Again signs on the same post.

"Mountain City's better," Eugene said.

Jeanette remembered riding on an escalator once when we were there.

Dad came about mid-morning that Saturday. Mom wanted to know when he'd have us back home.

"Fairly late," Dad said. There was a carnival in Mountain City and he thought we'd like to go to that.

"Yeaaa!" Jeanette said.

Mom looked concerned, but we assured her we would be all right. We rode to Mountain City and ate lunch in a restaurant. Afterward, as we were going back out on the street, Jeanette came running with a dollar in her hand. "Daddy, you forgot this!" she cried. Dad laughed, explained that it was a tip, and returned it to our table.

"Dummy," Eugene said to Jeanette as we walked to Dad's car.

Jeanette's face clouded.

Dad took Jeanette's hand and told Eugene not to say anything else to her. "You didn't know about a tip, did you?" he asked her.

Jeanette shook her head.

"But you do now!"

Jeanette nodded.

Dad picked Jeanette up and carried her in his arms the rest of the way to the car. We drove to the trout pond on Spring Creek, where about a hundred people were fishing. Actually, there were three blue ponds in a row, with a big tin-roofed shed, a little stand where people bought sandwiches and drinks, and another where they bought bait, and benches and tables in shady places. Summer people in bright Bermuda shorts, floppy hats, and sunglasses were fishing or sitting around on benches in the shade.

Dad talked to a man named Luther, who ran the bait stand and cleaned people's fish for them, and then to a young man with a blue tattoo on his forearm who ran the snack stand. I could tell from the way he talked to them that he was their boss. And when we fished, we didn't have to pay like everyone else. Dad got some rods from the shed and took us to the lower pond, where nobody else was fishing. Eugene and I cast little silver spinners out into the pond and reeled them in. Dad cast Jeanette's for her, then let her reel in. A trout struck her spinner, but the fish came up out of the water, shook its head, and got off the hook.

I was watching Dad and Jeanette when a trout struck my spinner and swam away, making my reel go *zzzz*. While I was standing there with my rod bent almost double, Eugene grunted and jerked his rod. A trout had struck his line, too.

When the fish were tired, we reeled them in. Dad said we'd turn these loose. Some other time, if we wanted to keep the trout we caught, we could. But we were going to the carnival that evening.

"Let's just feed the fish," Dad said. He brought a small bag of pellets and threw a handful into the water. Suddenly the water rippled, swirled, and then became a white froth as dozens of rainbow trout rose and chased the pellets. We each threw a handful of pellets and watched the trout fight over them. Jeanette rationed her pellets and threw one at a time until they were all gone.

After we'd had supper in another restaurant—Jeanette left the tip on the table this time—we drove out to the carnival. It was outside Mountain City in a huge field by the river. We could see the tents and the Ferris wheel from far away. Dad bought a whole roll of tickets and divided them up among us. We did just about everything: the merry-go-round, the bumper cars, the Wild Mouse, the House of Horrors. We threw baseballs and darts and shot a rifle at moving ducks. Eugene won a key ring throwing baseballs. I almost won something throwing darts but missed the last balloon. Dad won a fuzzy pink bear for Jeanette shooting the rifle. Jeanette carried the bear with her when we rode the Ferris wheel. She sat with Dad in the seat ahead of Eugene and me, the pink bear between them. Dad said there might be money to be made in a carnival. On the way back to Grandma and Grandpa Smith's, Jeanette fell asleep in the front seat of Dad's car, holding her bear. I sat in the back seat with Eugene and watched a full moon round as a silver dollar follow us all the way from Mountain City back to Newfound Creek.

~~~ ~~~

IN LATE AUGUST and early September Eugene and I helped cut the tobacco, working with Grandpa Smith afternoons after school. I was in seventh grade at Newfound School now, with Eugene two grades behind me, and Jeanette two grades behind him. We also helped Grandpa Smith and Coy Marler and Jess Woody make molasses. Grandpa Smith hitched Bertie to a long pole on the molasses mill, and Bertie walked around and around, turning the mill, pressing the sweet juice from the cane. Eugene tasted the dark syrup that remained after the juice had been boiled; it didn't make him sick the way the honey had.

Fall came. Leaves turned yellow and blazing red and began to rattle in the wind. The air turned crisp. Eugene, Jeanette, and I picked chinquapins on the hills afternoons after school. We gathered walnuts and got our hands stained yellow from the walnut hulls.

Our old life at home began to feel far away and long ago, even though the house we'd lived in was not far away. But that fall Grandpa Wells rented the house where we'd lived to Grady Plemmons, and that made me feel as if our life together there was really over. I stopped walking down there to sit on the hill and look at our old house.

When it was rainy and damp, later in the fall, and the tobacco hung cured to a golden color in the barn, we helped get it ready for market, separating the leaves into various grades, and tying them into bundles, using a folded tobacco leaf to wrap each bundle of about twenty leaves into a "hand."

Just before Thanksgiving Grandpa Smith slaughtered the largest of the three hogs in the big pen out by the barn. Coy Marler came to help. They hung the hog on a gambrel stick with a rope that worked on a pulley suspended from a tree limb. They lowered the hog into a big barrel of steaming water, raised it again, and scraped off the loose hair. Soon the hog was hams and shoulders and sausage in the smokehouse, and Eugene had the hog's bladder for a balloon.

In December Grandpa had the tobacco hauled to a warehouse in Jewell Hill, where it was sold at auction. Some of his fox-hunting cronies brought Grandpa Smith home from the tobacco sale. They had all sold their tobacco and were a little tipsy. I had never seen Grandpa Smith so cheerful, nor his wallet so full of money. But he had to give half the money to Grandpa Wells, Grandma Smith reminded him. She made him sit at the supper table and drink coffee until he wasn't as cheerful as he had been when he came home from Jewell Hill.

At night, in the back bedroom of Grandma and Grandpa's old gray house, with Eugene sleeping beside me, I would listen to sounds—cold creeping in, ice growing. And I could sense that the air was different one night when the first snow fell.

Riding the bus to Newfound School, early in the morning when the mountains looked like a black-and-white photograph in Grandma Smith's album, I would sit next to the window and look out at icicles hanging from rocks on the road bank. At school I noticed that I didn't like to hear anyone laughing; the sound was like glass breaking or ice cracking. Although I'd always liked my teachers, I resented their cheerfulness. Their smiles struck me like blinding sunlight. And always there was a cold place inside me, like frost on the shaded north side of the barn roof—a cold place that never melted, no matter how bright the day.

Sometimes I felt old and wise, like Grandma or Grandpa Smith. Ten minutes later I felt younger than Eugene or Jeanette. Down in December, as Christmas approached, I'd lie awake at night and fill the room with loud imaginings. Branches at the window, crooked and black against the ice-blue moon, became reindeer antlers clicking together, drawing the shadow of Santa Claus along the wall. Out of the pages of remembered books, camels strode, stately and aloof. Wise men jostled with elves, their faces all warts and whiskers, who chattered and sawed, and screeched and scurried about so noisily I thought surely they would wake Eugene, or else Mom or Grandma or Grandpa Smith would come to see why elves hummed and hammered in the room, or why camels were walking through the house. Then I would wish the whole house into a crèche—so still the only sounds were straw rustling, a lamb dreaming in baa, and the Christ Child sucking a tiny fist.

⇛ 11 ⇚

W E HAD TWO CHRISTMASES, one at Grandma and Grandpa Smith's, and another at Grandma and Grandpa Wells's, with trees and gifts in both places. But it was the gift Mom got herself that made the season come early: a brand-new portable typewriter in a green carrying case. One evening a few days before Christmas Carlene Cantrell helped Mom carry several bags in from the car when they got home from Blue Ridge Manufacturing. Our gifts, I figured. Mom and Carlene carried everything straight back to Mom's room. But then Carlene stayed a few minutes while Mom brought the typewriter out of her room into the kitchen, took it out of the case, and set it on the table.

"That thing would buffalo me," Carlene said, her round face beaming. "But your mom, she'll be going lickety-split on it in no time. I tell you, your mom's something else! She got her diploma! Did she tell you?"

Mom hadn't told us because she hadn't actually received the diploma yet.

"But you've finished all the work, and passed everything," Carlene said. "That's what counts."

Carlene said when Mom learned to type, she would get a better job in the plant—as a secretary to Walter Lee Rogers. If Mom kept up, she'd soon be head of it all there at Blue Ridge Manufacturing! She said she hoped we were proud of Mom.

We said we were.

"Your mom took this manual dexterity test at work," Carlene said, "and, why, just shot the moon on it! They say she made higher on that test than anybody that's ever worked there."

"I'm all right as long as I don't tense up," Mom said. "I didn't even know it was a test I was taking. If I'd known, I would have done awful."

I was proud she made so high on the manual dexterity test, and glad she had the new typewriter. I'd liked typewriters ever since I'd been in the third grade and my teacher had let me type on hers. I showed Mom how to set the margins and lock down the keys to make all capital letters. I typed "Now is the time for all good men to come to the aid of their party" and the bell on the typewriter rang.

After Carlene went on home, Mom took the typewriter and the warranty papers back to the bedroom. She had a little payment book, too, for making the monthly fourteen-dollar payments. I was dying to use the typewriter, but she practiced on it all evening, doing the first exercises in a book she'd also bought. I could hear her clacking away: asdf   jkl; asdf   jkl;   asdf   jkl;. Then the bell would ring and she would start all over.

In January Mom's high-school diploma came in the mail from Nashville. It was an "equivalency" diploma, but Mom said it was just as good as if it had come from a real school. She framed it and hung it up in Jeanette's and her bedroom, over the table where she had worked so many hours, and where now she also had the chart of the typewriter keyboard.

When she started learning, the sounds of the typewriter in her bedroom were slow and methodical: *clack clack, clack clack—clack, clack, clack, clack*. But in a couple of weeks, just as Carlene Cantrell said, Mom was picking up speed and pretty soon she was going *clackety-clackety-clackety ding, clackety-clackety-clackety ding*.

"Mom has manual dexterity," Jeanette told us. "But she's not a man—hummph!"

Mom was getting far along in the book, typing whole paragraphs, keeping track of her speed, counting her mistakes. She was using up lots of typing paper.

At supper one evening I said Dad's sister, our Aunt Vi the college teacher, typed the letters she sent to Grandma Wells. I had seen some of them, and they were typed neatly.

Mom cocked her head to one side. "I wonder if your grandma Wells knows how to type," she said, and the corners of her mouth moved as if she were going to say something else. But she didn't.

⇶ 12 ⇷

I LISTENED TO MOM, and I'd ask Dad questions when he came by on Sundays to take Jeanette and Eugene and me down to Grandma and Grandpa Wells's. Remembering how it had been, living together in our own house, I realized now that I'd never known we were a family, or even thought about it, until we weren't any longer. The family had always just been there, even when Mom and Dad argued and I'd be upset. The family was there like the sun and air, as unshakable as trees on the mountains all around. But now that Mom and Dad had separated, it was as if the trees had been uprooted and torn from the mountains, as if the mountains had been cut up and scarred, their tops thrown into the valleys, like the mountains that had been strip-mined over in Bunker County.

Now I had a craving to know everything about our family, and I found out a lot of things I hadn't known before. I began really to look at Grandma and Grandpa Wells's house when we went there, and to think about it. There was a road like a tunnel. Tall white pines lined both sides of it, growing together overhead, shutting out the light. And at the end of the road stood the two-story house, surrounded by cedars. Massive rosebushes crept untended over the yard, up the latticework of the porch, and along the iron handrail beside the steps. Out of sight in the cedars, sparrows chirped, and off in the garden or down by the creek, peacocks shrieked. The chirping sparrows and the shrieking peacocks were a Sunday sound to me.

That winter, when Dad would come get us and take us down to Grandma and Grandpa Wells's, I'd slip away and prowl the second story of the house, in rooms, shut off for years, that had a musty smell hinting of mysteries. I found old books in tiny print, by Milton and Tennyson; a washstand with pitcher and bowl done in white colored etchings; pictures in dust-laden, oval frames of stern, stiff-necked men and tight-lipped women in long black dresses with bustles. I found a violin in a dusty black case, that I would take out and try to play. There were big trunks with more books, pictures, letters, old newspapers, and magazines.

I'd sit in a chair by the window and look down toward Sextons', or up the creek toward Grandma and Grandpa Smith's, over the fallow bottomland and hillside fields where tobacco and corn grew in spring and summer. When I was younger, it had never occurred to me to wonder why Grandma and Grandpa Wells owned the farm and Grandma and Grandpa Smith only lived on it and worked for shares—why Grandma Wells's hands were small and white but Grandma Smith's were large and brown, or why Grandma Smith had chickens and guineas and Grandpa Smith had a pack of foxhounds, while Grandma and Grandpa Wells had peacocks. It all seemed to me then as natural as the familiar fields.

There was a time when I'd been fascinated with Grandpa Wells's binoculars, and when we went there I'd take them upstairs and look at Velma, the strange woman who played on the porch down at Sextons'. I don't remember how I knew about Velma. I must have heard Mom and Dad talk about her, or Grandma and Grandpa Wells. At the time, I thought I'd discovered her.

One afternoon Dad came upstairs to see what I was doing and found me looking down toward Sextons' through the binoculars. He took them, and, looking at Velma on the porch, he told me about her. She was older than he was, but when she was younger, she had been allowed to play with other children, and he remembered Velma used to go with the kids around there picking chinquapins and gathering walnuts. They'd crack walnuts and feed them to Velma, as if she were a puppy. Velma had never gone to school. Before she was old enough to go, she'd been afflicted.

I thought about her name. Velma. It was all right for a grown woman. Grown people had names like that. Vergie. Vergil. J. D. Marler's grandmother, who lived with the Marlers on Grandpa Wells's farm, was named Vashti. But I couldn't imagine a little girl named Velma going with other kids to gather walnuts or pick chinquapins.

But Velma had been her name, even when she was a little girl. She'd almost died—with meningitis, Dad said—when she was about five, and her mind had never developed beyond that age. That was why she played with dolls and chewed sticks, although she was older than my father. That was why the Sextons had an expandable gate at the top of the porch steps—to keep Velma from falling down the steps, or maybe wandering off.

Dad wrapped the strap around the binoculars.

"Let me have them back!" I said.

"No. You've got no business looking at Velma that way."

"Why not?"

"It's not a thing to do."

After that, Dad wouldn't let me take the binoculars upstairs. But I'd go up there anyway and prowl the rooms and sit among the old trunks, surrounded by those stern faces in their oval frames, and think about things Dad or Mom or Grandma or Grandpa Wells had told me. I remembered that Mom and Dad had lived upstairs here until I was a year old. My whole life—all our lives—seemed strange. Sitting by the window, I'd try to play the old violin, bringing forth tuneless sounds that lingered, hanging like dust in a shaft of light. At times the sounds I made on the violin put me in mind of the peacocks' screeching; at others, of Grandma Smith's guineas when they were excited or frightened. But always the silence in those rooms seemed to whisper things about the farm, and all of us living there.

Grandpa Wells inherited the farm from his father. The Wellses and the Reeveses—Grandma Wells had been a Reeves before she married—were important people in the county and always had been. Grandma Wells told me that. Besides Grandma and Grandpa Smith, there were two other families on the farm who worked for shares—the Marlers and the Woodys. And sometimes there'd be others who stayed a year or two and then moved on.

Grandpa Smith hadn't had any land. He and Grandma Smith had lived on a lot of farms in east Tennessee, staying one crop-year here, another year or two there, and then moving on, always looking for a better house, a better share. When their children were at home—Uncle Clint, Aunt

Frances, Van, Ray, Joe, Lon, and Mom, who was the youngest—they'd lived in a succession of sharecropper houses. From what Grandma Smith told me, I had a general picture of all of them. She'd have some flowers in tin buckets on the porch. There'd be a springhouse, pole barn, smokehouse, garden, a woodyard with stacks of stovewood drying, chicken coops, doghouses, chickens cackling, guineas pottericking, dogs yelping.

They kept moving, year after year, always to a new place that was always the same place. Finally, after most of their children had grown up and moved away, but when Mom was just a baby, they moved to Grandma and Grandpa Wells's farm—and had lived there ever since.

So Mom and Dad grew up right on the same farm, but not together, Mom said. Dad was six years older than she was, and, besides, she lived up in the holler and was just another one of the sharecropper kids, like the Marler and Woody children. The way Dad told it, they "met" once, as if they'd never seen one another before.

Dad had been squirrel hunting and he came out of the woods where Grandpa Smith was coming along the wagon road with a load of corn. He stepped up on the side of the wagon and stood there, hitching a ride, his rifle slung over his shoulder. He had ridden along a good piece before he looked down in the wagon and saw Mom sitting there, in the corner, her oval face framed by her straight black hair. Just about that time the wagon wheel hit a chuckhole, the wagon lurched, and Dad lost his toehold and fell off. As he hit the ground, he heard Mom laugh. Dad said he leaped back onto the wagon and wedged his toes in good between the sideboards. And when he looked down at Mom that time, she seemed to draw further back into the corner. She was wearing a necklace made out of round, black chinquapins strung on sewing thread, he recollected, and that was the first time he had ever really paid much attention to her.

Dad said he rode all the way to the barn and helped Grandpa Smith and Mom unload the corn. After that, he saw Mom trying to fill a bucket at a pump behind the house. She worked the pump handle up and down, but no water came. "You have to prime it," he told her. "Oh," she said, and began pumping again as fast as she could. So he primed the pump and ran the bucket full while she looked on. They talked. He guessed she was—what?—twelve or thirteen years old. She gave him to know she was sixteen! Sixteen —that was old enough to go places, Dad said. Mom said she went to church, and she named the church. "They're Holy Rollers," Dad said. But that was where they went on their first date.

Not long after that, they drove to Kentucky on a Saturday afternoon and got married.

⇶ 13 ⇷

GRANDMA WELLS TALKED to me differently now. At least, I thought she did. I used to be a little afraid around her, and stiff, but that was probably because I knew Mom didn't like her. Now, though, I was spending a lot of time down at her house and getting to know her on my own. Mom had told me all the bad things Grandma Wells had done to her, but she was always good to me. I got so I loved to talk to her. She told me a lot of things about Dad and Aunt Vi and Aunt Alma, his sisters, and his older brothers, Herbert and Arnold—things I had never known.

"You're no longer a child, Robert," she said to me one afternoon when I walked down to her house after school. "If you want to be more than a field hand, you should be thinking about what you want to become. You appear to be bright enough." Grandma Wells was short and fine-boned, with short gray hair and sharp features. If she'd had a ruffled collar, she would have looked like Queen Elizabeth, whose picture was in our seventh-grade literature book at school.

I didn't know what to say. "I don't have any trouble in school. I like it." I told her how Miss Briggs had let me type on her typewriter when I was in third grade, and how, last year, Mrs. Merrill had let me go to the other classrooms at Newfound School and tell the class stories. I told some stories from the schoolbooks, like the one about the yellow tiger that ran around and around the tree until it melted into butter. But I also told stories Grandpa Smith told me, like the one about the squirrel that stole corn and ferried it back to its nest on the other side of the creek by floating the ear of corn on a shingle and paddling with its tail.

She said public speaking was good experience. "Your father always did well in school." She sighed. Dad had gone two years to college and then quit, she said. He had just recently come home from college, I figured out, that time he stepped up on the side of Grandpa Smith's corn wagon and looked down in it and saw Mom. "Your father just turned his back on advantages," Grandma Wells said. "I've never understood it. I hope you won't do that."

"Yes, ma'am. I mean—" I didn't want to say I hoped I'd do better than Dad.

She told me about her school days. She had gone to a blab school when she was a little girl, a school where all the little scholars studied everything out loud, learned it by heart, and then presented recitations on Friday afternoons.

I said we still did things like that at Newfound School. Last year Mrs. Merrill had taken some of us to Jewell Hill and we were on the radio for a program about Abraham Lincoln. I'd memorized "O Captain, My Captain!" and said it on the radio.

Grandma Wells wished she had known about it. She would have listened. She could recite all sorts of poems, and songs, and speeches, and what she called recitation pieces. She recited Kipling's "If" to me, and embarrassed me. "If you can keep your head when all about you / Are losing theirs . . . you'll be a Man, my son!"

"Yes, ma'am," I said.

After blab school she had gone a year to the old Jewell Hill Academy, for culture and refinement. Grandpa Wells had gone to an academy, too, the Barnard Academy. The Reeveses and the Wellses always had been people who believed in education. They were of the better class of people, the good livers. There were two classes of people, she said, the good livers and the sorry.

I wanted to know more about the difference between them.

Good livers were workers, she explained. They looked ahead, laid up for a rainy day. They were good providers.

And the sorry?

The sorry were shiftless, didn't look ahead. They were improvident, lived from hand to mouth.

A person should have goals, ambitions. Grandma Wells hoped I had goals.

I assured her I did. I didn't say, though, that I wasn't exactly sure what they were.

Now, Dad's sisters had goals. They were the only ones among Grandma Wells's children who had really pursued goals. Aunt Vi was a teacher in a college in Pennsylvania. And Alma had gone into the theater and was having right much success in a theatrical career. Uncle Arnold, Dad's oldest brother, had done the same kind of thing Dad did —dropped out of college and gone to work in the automobile tire business. Now he sold cars in St. Augustine, Florida. Uncle Herbert had made a career out of the military service, and lived in Cherry Point, North Carolina.

"Dad won a speech contest once," I said. "And a medal."

"Yes, he did," Grandma Wells agreed. "And he could have gone on to such fine things, if only he'd had a mind to. But no, instead he—"

I hoped she wasn't thinking that instead of doing something fine, Dad had married Mom.

She changed the subject, and talked about the importance of one's people. "Your fifth great-grandparents on your father's side, George Palmer and Elizabeth Wyatt, were born in England," she said. They had come to Virginia, where they married and raised a family. They had sons who fought in the American Revolution. "Several of your ancestors— the Palmers, the Wellses, and the Reeveses—served in the Revolution, and on both sides in the Civil War."

She got out a big chart showing a family tree with red, brown, and green branches. It looked like a big oak tree that had been cut down in England and fallen into the Atlantic Ocean. But I noticed that some of our ancestors came from Scotland, and Ireland, and Germany. And some had come from Pennsylvania, not Virginia. I wondered if that was why Aunt Vi taught in Pennsylvania.

Grandma Wells gave me a book of poems and challenged me to memorize some of them. She said every time I came to her house, she wanted me to be able to recite her a new one. She gave me some copies of *National Geographic*. She hoped I was learning about the wider world. It wasn't good to have a narrow view of the world. One had to be able to see further than the holler one lived in.

I agreed.

I took the book of poems and the *National Geographic* magazines and walked up the holler to Grandma and Grandpa Smith's. I wondered if Grandma Wells thought that Grandma and Grandpa Smith belonged to the sorry people. If she did, she was wrong, because they weren't shiftless; they worked, and they worked hard. I still couldn't understand the difference between the better class of people, the good livers, and the sorry.

$\gg 14 \ll$

I SAT IN THE kitchen clear into spring, in the corner by the woodstove, and read my book of poems and asked Grandma Smith questions. She didn't know as much about her ancestors as Grandma Wells did. She didn't have a chart.

"All of them come from across the waters, back years ago, I reckon," she said.

But she did tell me a lot of things I hadn't known. Grandpa Smith's people had been Black Dutch, she'd always heard him say. Grandpa Smith had been married before he married her, she told me. I hadn't known that.

Oh, yes. His first wife died with the measles. Back in those days people died with measles, flu, pneumonia. Left him with two little children.

Really?

"Yes, your Uncle Van and your Uncle Ray are your Grandpa Smith's children by his first wife. They're your mother's half-brothers. Only Clint and Joe and Lon and your aunt Frances are her full brothers and sister. Dolly died. Fred Steven died."

I hadn't know that, either.

Hoeing with her in the garden, I asked her how she and Grandpa Smith had met.

Grandma Smith smiled remembering. She had been coming out of church, and Grandpa Smith was standing there. He wasn't a stranger to her. She knew him. She'd known his wife, Odessa, who had died and left him with two small children, one just a baby. There'd been a big pile of wood there close to the church, and Grandpa Smith motioned to it as she walked by and called her by her first name. " 'Kate,' he said, 'I'd chop that whole pile of wood for the chance to walk you home.' "

"Did you make him chop the wood?"

"Why, no! That was just his way of talkin'."

"You let him walk you home without choppin' the wood?"

"Yes."

"And then you got married."

"Well, not just like that. But it wasn't long."

Grandma Smith had two pictures in oval frames hanging in the house. One was a picture of a bearded man with his hair parted in the middle. That was her father's brother, Alfred Ponder. The other was of a woman, seated, and another bearded man, standing behind the woman with his hand on her shoulder. They were her mother and father, Leland and Irene Ponder. Her mother had been a Weaver.

"Are those all the pictures we have?" I asked.

There were some others in a little album, and still others in the back of the Bible.

"There is one other," she said, "behind Mama and Papa."

I studied my great-grandfather Leland there in his oval frame, his hand on the back of a chair. He had a black beard, black hat, black Sunday coat, and he stood looking as if he knew something I didn't.

Grandma Smith took the picture down off the wall and told me what she had found years ago. Once, when she'd been cleaning the frame, she'd taken her parents' picture out and found behind it a second picture, an old tintype.

She took the back off the frame, removed the tintype, and showed it to me: a cloudy face, little more than a shadow.

"Who is it?" I asked.

Grandma Smith didn't know. She said the picture had been in there for years before she found it by accident.

Was it one of our ancestors?

She didn't know. It might be. Then again, it might just be an old picture that was in the frame when they bought it. It could be anybody.

I looked at the dim tintype, then at my great-grandfather Leland. "They look alike, a little."

Grandma Smith had thought so too, but nobody knew for sure. She put the old tintype back in the frame and hung it on the wall.

"Could I look at him again sometime?"

I could, if I'd be careful with the frame, and not break the glass.

Sometimes, when no one else was in the house, I'd go in Grandma Smith's room and stand looking at great-grandfather Leland and thinking about the picture behind his, pressed like a leaf between pages of a book. I'd take the picture down, remove the back, and take the tintype out and study it. The more I studied the face, the more it seemed he could be anyone. I couldn't even be certain it was a man; it might have been a woman. I'd put the picture back in the frame and hang it on the wall and think of the person, whoever he was, whoever she was. The picture made me think of all those people, as many as leaves on all the trees in the yard, who had flourished, withered, and fallen to the ground.

The oval-framed pictures on the walls down at Grandma and Grandpa Wells's were my ancestors, too, and Grandma Wells could tell me exactly who they were. But I didn't feel the same way about them as I did about the person in the tintype on the wall at Grandma and Grandpa Smith's —not even about Robert Wells, the great-great-uncle who had been mayor of Jewell Hill and for whom I was named.

When I read my book of poems or looked at the people in the *National Geographics*, I'd sometimes find myself thinking of the person in the tintype behind my great-grandfather Leland's picture, about how the person could be an Indian, or an African, or an Arab. The picture was so dim, all you could see was a human person. Without telling anyone, I claimed the unknown person as a kinsman, a life behind my life. To be closer, sometimes I'd stand close to the oval frame and cloud the glass with my breath.

WE DIDN'T BUY as many groceries out of the store after we moved to Grandma and Grandpa Smith's. They raised almost all their food. There were potatoes stored in a big cone-shaped mound, beneath straw. We had dried apples, ham and sausage from the smokehouse, and vegetables fresh from the garden or canned. Grandma Smith had a can house that was dug back into the side of the hill. It was always cool in summer and warm in winter. She raised two rows of popcorn in the garden, and Eugene, Jeanette, and I popped popcorn on the woodstove in the living room.

In early spring, when pussy willows were budding along the branch bank, Mom went with us to gather cresses. She said she had gathered cresses on that same branch bank when she was a little girl. She made a salad from the cresses that tasted better than the lettuce we used to get from the store.

Grandma Smith wanted to plant potatoes on Good Friday, but Grandpa Smith didn't have the ground quite ready, so we planted potatoes the next day. Grandma Smith said Good Friday was the best time to plant. Good Saturday was close enough, Grandpa Smith said. Eugene, Jeanette, and I helped. Mom stayed in the house and typed things she'd brought home from work. Grandma Smith showed us how to recognize the seed potatoes' "eyes," and how to cut them up so that each piece had an eye. The piece of potato wouldn't sprout and make a plant, she said, unless it had an eye.

"If they have eyes, can they see?" Jeanette asked.

Grandma Smith said potatoes had eyes but they couldn't see. Neither could a needle, and a needle had an eye.

"A shoe's got a tongue, but it can't talk," Eugene said. He drew eyebrows over two eyes of a potato, and a mouth and nose, and held it up for us to see. Jeanette had to draw a potato face, too.

After Grandpa Smith had the potato patch laid off in rows, we each took a row, carrying a pail of cut-up seed potatoes, and walked along dropping the pieces into the furrow about a foot apart. We stepped on each piece, pressing it down into the loose soil. Then Grandpa came along with Bertie hitched to a plow and covered the potatoes in the furrow.

15

GRANDPA SMITH'S OVERALLS hung loosely on him, and there was so much slack in the seat of them that his back pockets overlapped. His ears were fuzzy and gray hairs grew out of them, like mistletoe on the old oak tree above the barn. He smelled of sheep dip, for he was always treating his foxhounds for mange.

When I was thirteen, he was seventy-one. When we worked in the tobacco field in June, hoeing it, and later, in July, pulling the sticky green suckers from the plants, he'd hold the water jar to his lips and his hand would tremble. If he got too hot, he had dizzy spells. I'd always known he talked to himself when he worked, but I never paid any attention to what he said until one day when we were resting on the creek bank at the edge of the tobacco field. Grandpa Smith fanned himself slowly with his hat and said, "By the waters of Babylon, there sat we down . . ."

I looked around. He was gazing off down the creek.

From then on, I listened when he talked to himself. One evening we went fox hunting, and when we'd climbed to the top of Horse Knob and sat down to listen to the hounds chase a fox, he said something about a place "where the wicked cease from troubling, and the weary be at rest."

What he said reminded me of some of the poems I'd been learning from the book Grandma Wells had given me back in the winter. After the hounds had struck the trail of a fox and gone out of hearing over the next ridge, the night was still except for a slight breeze in the oak tree we were sitting under. The moon overhead looked like a print of yellow butter. I thought of the beginning of a poem in my book and said it:

> *"The old moon is tarnished*
> *With smoke of the flood,*
> *The new moon is varnished*
> *With color like blood."*

"Where'd you hear that?" Grandpa Smith asked.

"Read it—in a book. It's a poem."

"Now say that again."

I did. He listened, and then he said it. It sounded a lot better when he said it. When he said words like "moon" and "smoke" and "blood," I saw the things in my mind.

I wrote a poem that summer, the second summer we lived at Grandma and Grandpa Smith's. He had given me a pup right after Mom moved us there. The pup didn't turn out to be a big dog, but when she was growing up she never was skinny or long-legged as most dogs are. She'd sit in the dog lot with the other Walker foxhounds and look like a statue of a dog, spotted a pale yellow, a brown streak blazing her forehead. Grandpa Smith called her "that little lemon bitch." I named her Lady, because she never hogged her food down in chunks. She had manners. The poem I wrote, and typed on Mom's typewriter, was about my dog, Lady. It started out:

Thou still unravished little lemon bitch—

In August I helped Grandpa Smith cut tobacco. We took our time because it was so hot, and rested at the end of each long row. Grandpa Smith would sit fanning himself with his old black hat. I'd pull out my poetry book and read something. I remember when I read:

Out of the night that covers me
Black as the pit from pole to pole
I thank whatever gods may be
For my unconquerable soul.

Grandpa Smith's hat moved slowly before his face. I got a whiff of sheep dip. "Black is the pit from pole to pole," he said.

"Black *as* the pit," I said.

"I think whatever gods may be," he said.

"No, it's 'I *thank* whatever gods'—like, thank you, gods." I read for him:

Under the wide and starry sky
Dig the grave and let me die.
. . . .
Home is the sailor, home from the sea,
And the hunter home from the hill.

I heard him say the line about the hunter once when he came back from Horse Knob. But he liked best the poems about the tarnished moon and the night as black as the pit. I read some poems from my book that didn't rhyme, like "When I Heard the Learned Astronomer" and "Patterns." He'd listen, but he let me know he didn't think much of them. He called them doo-dads.

I read him a poem about the unclean spirits that entered a herd of swine and made the hogs run over a cliff.

Grandpa Smith nodded. "I've heard that, and I'll tell you what it puts me in mind of." And he told about something that happened when he was a boy, squirrel hunting back in a place called the Bearwallow. He heard something coming at him through the woods. At first it sounded like a far-off waterfall. But he knew the woods, and there was no waterfall anywhere close by. Besides, while he stood still, the roar came closer—a curious noise, a rustling and a rushing and a whooshing in the leaves of the trees back there on the Bearwallow.

He thought maybe a storm was about to overtake him, and the coming rush was wind and rain whipping treetops. But the afternoon was still and sunny. Then he thought maybe it was hogs feeding on new-fallen acorns, for it was September. Or it could be cattle making a noise coming down the ridge.

He raised his rifle as the noise overtook him and he saw—gray squirrels, hundreds of them, coming through treetops down the ridge back. Gray squirrels leaped from limb to limb through chestnuts, oaks, and hickories, falling from one limb, grabbing hold on a lower one, some dropping, tearing down through leaves, thumping the ground like apples, recovering, scurrying back up the trunks of chestnuts and shagbark hickories, following the down-ridge flow—a river of gray squirrels running down the mountain. He couldn't say how long they were in passing, but however long it took, he'd stood there, his rifle raised, "and never shot a shoot," he said. "You put me in mind of that when you told about the hogs going over the cliff. I hadn't thought of that for years. I never saw anything like it before, or since."

Sometimes Grandpa Smith kidded me and told me tall tales, like the one about the catfish that was so big he had to fish for it with a hook made at the blacksmith shop, a line made from a plowline, and an anvil for a sinker. Or about the great coon dog that would catch a coon with a skin just the size of whatever stretching board Grandpa'd show it. Sadly, the dog disappeared into the woods and never returned after Grandma Smith set the ironing board out on the porch one evening. The story about the squirrels was a tale like that, I figured, so I said, "That never happened!"

"Oh, yes," he said. "It happened—years ago."

We went fox hunting on Horse Knob one evening after we'd cut tobacco all day. The next morning, a hot morning in late August, Lady was not in the lot with the other foxhounds. She had never failed to come home after a hunt before. I took Grandpa Smith's horn, climbed the hill above the barn, and blew for her. We had already cut a big square out of the tobacco patch, but the rows of uncut tobacco stood greenish silver with dew. I caught a movement at the edge of the patch, far below me, then watched Lady drag a green swath through the wet weeds with her belly. I ran down the hill toward her. Not until she was at my feet did I notice the swollen lump, swinging like a rotten tomato from the loose skin at her throat.

I called Grandpa Smith from the barn. He unbuckled the wet collar, now tight around Lady's neck because of the swelling. Taking the lump in his hand, he felt it gently, revealing the two red punctures, half an inch apart, that gaped through the short white hair on Lady's throat. He said one word: "Copperhead."

Lady shivered. Her small body was wet and skinny, her face was puffed.

"She won't die, will she?" I asked.

Grandpa Smith raised Lady's head and looked at her eyes. They were swollen almost shut. He didn't answer me.

"I'll doctor her," I said. I started to pick Lady up.

"Leave her alone," Grandpa Smith said.

"But she'll die."

"Leave her alone. Let her go off someplace."

"Go off and die!" I said. I hollered at him, "Let her go off and die!" I kicked at a fencepost.

Grandpa Smith looked straight at me. "Now, listen here, Mister Man, you'd best calm down, right now." He stepped between me and Lady.

She stood a minute, her head down. Then she turned and crept down to the creek, stiff-legged and hump-backed, like a sore-eyed cat. She was going off to die.

When the sun dried the tobacco off, we started our third day of cutting and hauling the tobacco to the barn—on a sled pulled by the mule, Bertie. I cut and Grandpa Smith strung the stalks of tobacco on sticks stuck upright in the ground. We never said a word all the way out the row. I'd come to a stalk I couldn't slice off with one pull of the knife and he'd stand there, rubbing his hands together, impatient, while I hacked away at the tough stalk.

We finished the row. I walked down to the creek to see about Lady. I found her stretched out under a clump of willows and got a coldness in the pit of my stomach, for I knew she was dead.

She wasn't dead, but she was so sick she paid no attention to me. She wouldn't look up at me or move at all. She just lay there, her neck resting in the mud.

"Let's go," Grandpa Smith said, just loud enough for me to hear. He was standing up on the creek bank whetting the tobacco knife with a stone he carried in his pocket.

At lunch, before I could get up from the table and go see about Lady, he said he needed to send me down to Grandpa Wells's store. "I need some tenpenny nails," he said. He had decided we needed to enlarge a temporary scaffolding where we hung the sticks of tobacco before putting them inside the barn.

I took the five-dollar bill he handed me. "Could I get some—linament, or something?"

"Your back sore?"

"No, but—for Lady. It might—"

"Just nails. Two pounds. And hurry back."

I stuck the money in my pocket and went out, slamming the screen door hard. I dawdled, just because Grandpa Smith had told me to hurry. But the road under my bare feet was hot and I had to go faster than I wanted to, or else walk in the sharp rocks on the road's edge. At the store I pitched two games of horseshoes with Clyde and Columbus Cox, knowing Grandpa Smith was waiting on me.

When I returned with the nails, he was sitting in a split-bottom chair in the front yard, in the shade of the big maple.

I dropped the nails on the grass beside him and started walking down toward the creek. I could feel him watching me all the way to the creek bank.

Then I knew why. Lady was gone. There was just a slick-looking, rolled-out place in the mud under the willow where she had lain.

I climbed back up the creek bank, a little sick. But I wasn't mad at Grandpa Smith anymore. I was glad he had carried Lady off while I was gone, because I didn't want to see her. Just to show him I wasn't mad at him, I walked under the maple and sat down in the shade not far from him.

"You take a dog," Grandpa Smith said, "you can always notice, if a dog is snakebit, it'll go to a branch bank or a creek bank, and lay in the mud. I've seen 'em do it, many's the time."

I didn't want to hear about it. I stretched out face down on the grass and tried to keep from thinking about that slick-looking, rolled-out place in the mud where Lady had lain.

"Now, if one ever gets up from that mud it lays in, why then it's all right, generally," Grandpa Smith said. "And I reckon that little lemon bitch will live."

I jumped up and looked around.

" 'Home is the hunter,' " he said, grinning.

"What? Where?"

"She come up out of the creek and went to the lot," he said.

I started for the lot, but Grandpa Smith said, "Just leave her alone. Let her rest. She'll get over a snake bite, but you're apt to love her to death."

I felt two ways at once—good because Lady was going to live, bad because I'd hollered at Grandpa Smith and slammed the screen door hard. I sat on the shaded grass beside him, looking off toward the dog lot in the pines. "You never saw squirrels coming through the trees like that, did you? That's just something you made up or heard, something like, 'The Assyrian came down like the wolf on the fold.' "

"It happened," he said.

⋙ 16 ⋘

OUR NEWFOUND SCHOOL CLOSED. Mom and Grandma and Grandpa Smith were against the school closing, but Grandma and Grandpa Wells said it was probably for the best. So I started eighth grade at West Madison Consolidated. All the students who lived on Newfound Creek still rode the same yellow school bus, number 74, but now we rode farther, and to a big school where everything was new to us—new teachers, new classmates.

Two or three days after school started that September, Miss Hudspeth, the school nurse, her white uniform swishing and crackling like stiff new overalls, came to our room during math class. Bending over a little beside our teacher, Miss Merit, who was sitting at her desk, Miss Hudspeth picked a long blond hair off Miss Merit's blue blouse, and as she let it fall to the floor, she whispered something into Miss Merit's ear. Miss Merit made an O with her mouth. Miss Hudspeth squinted out at us from the glare of her smile, then whispered something else to Miss Merit, who nodded up and down.

The nurse came around in front of Miss Merit's desk and took a pencil from the suddenly limp hand of a girl who had been absently biting into the soft yellow wood. She laid the pencil in the tray on the desk and asked, "How many little Newfound folk are in this eighth-grade room? Raise your hands, please."

There were three of us—J. D. Marler, Mack Woody, and I.

Miss Merit scooted her chair back and said, "Robert, J. D., Mack, go with Miss Hudspeth."

We looked at one another. Our classmates turned in their seats and stared at us. And I was suddenly feverish with shame, not for anything I had done—I didn't know what the nurse wanted with us—but because I was from Newfound.

We stepped to the front of the room and had started to follow Miss Hudspeth out the door when she turned back to say something else to Miss Merit. As they talked, her hands absently gripped my head and pressed it down against my chest. All the time she was standing there reminding Miss Merit of a film on nutrition to be shown in the gym on Friday, her hard, dry fingers—they smelled of alcohol —were busy in my hair, mussing it this way and that.

Miss Hudspeth took us to the gym, where Jeanette and Selma Austin and three other girls who rode the Newfound bus were already waiting on the gray bleachers. Eugene, who was a sixth-grader now, was already there, too; he had taken off his new shoes and was running around in his new socks, sliding on the smooth gym floor. J. D. Marler and Mack Woody took off their shoes and slid, too.

Miss Hudspeth kept coming back with two or three boys and girls who rode the Newfound bus until she had all of us. Then she made the boys stop sliding and put on their shoes, and had us sit on the bleachers, the boys in one group, the girls in another. She walked out onto the gym floor, turned to us, clasped her hands together in front of her as if she were thankful for something, and began to talk—her voice echoing in the gym—about head lice, about how it was no disgrace to have them, yet there was no excuse for not getting rid of them.

Before we went back to our rooms, we had to line up in front of Miss Hudspeth's office, which was right beside the gym, and go in one at a time and find out if we had head lice. My head itched where she had mussed my hair. Before my turn came to go in, I felt as if lice were crawling not only on my head but all over me. I just wanted to get on the yellow bus, go home, and never come back to West Madison Consolidated School. I hadn't wanted to come in the first place.

My turn came. Miss Hudspeth closed the door behind us, walked me over to the window, and as she looked in my hair again, I rested my hands on the table between a cold white enamel pan of disinfectant with thermometers submerged in it and a box of wooden tongue depressors. I waited to be condemned. But she said, "You're all right," gripped my shoulder, and turned me away from the window. "But you should wash your hair more often." She opened the door and motioned me out. I couldn't believe all she had found was a little dirt.

That afternoon on the school bus, as we sat squeezed in beside each other, we knew somebody who rode our bus must have head lice, but we still didn't know who it was.

My sister Jeanette and all the other girls were very quiet. Selma Austin sat with her notebook in her lap, her pretty smooth hands folded on the notebook. J. D. Marler held his hand over her head and clicked his fingernails. "Cootie, cootie!" he said. Selma told him to stop it. Then I told him to stop it. But he kept on pestering her, clicking his fingernails, pretending he was finding head lice in her hair. Selma began to cry. I frogged the muscle in his arm with my fist. He didn't do anything for a minute; then, when I was looking at Selma, he whunked me in the chest as hard as he could, and I hit him back, right in the forehead with my fist, so hard I thought I'd broken my hand. Mr. Garrett, the bus driver, stopped the bus and told us we'd have to walk home if we didn't stop fighting. He didn't allow fighting on his bus. I looked J.D. Marler right in the eye, and he looked me right in the eye, but we didn't do anything else.

Mr. Garrett drove on until we came to the bad bridge, where he stopped to let us all out so he could drive the bus empty across the rickety old thing. As soon as we got off, J. D. Marler hit me a couple of licks on the shoulder. We were standing on the side of the road circling each other, trying to get in a good lick, when Mr. Garrett closed the school-bus door and drove off without us. We didn't fight any more. J. D. climbed the road bank and went over the hill toward his house. I stayed on the road and walked home in about fifteen minutes.

The next morning when I got on the bus, Mr. Garrett said, "I see you two banty roosters didn't peck each other to death." And every boy who got on the bus as we rode down the Newfound Creek road had something smart to say about J. D. and me having to walk home. Selma Austin sat with her pretty hands folded on her notebook. J. D. and his little brother Carl did not catch the bus that morning. Mack Woody stood up in the aisle and shouted that it was J. D. and Carl who had the cooties, and everyone agreed. Later we found out for sure, that Mack had been right.

When J. D. failed to answer roll call that morning, there was a sudden shuffling, twisting, whispering, and snickering that Miss Merit ignored. The others knew, or at least they suspected. And they suspected Mack and me, because we were from Newfound, too. While I was reading, I saw one girl whispering to another, and looking at me. I lost my place. Later that day I looked up from my math book and saw a big-shouldered, blond-haired boy looking at me while making a motion with his fingers of little feet running through his hair. When he saw me looking at him, he pretended to be scratching his head absently. The boy beside him grew red in the face from holding back a snicker. I sat gripping my book until its covers were sweaty under my fingers.

At recess I walked the playground among the teeming, screaming rope-skippers and marble-shooters. Somebody sang, "Ask me no questions and I'll tell you no lice!" And I walked the halls, for all I wanted to do was to keep moving and act as if I were going somewhere.

West Madison was very modern, bright and colorful. There were skylights in the rooms and halls; smooth tiled floors, which the janitors swept with green sawdust; pink, yellow, and green rooms; desks arranged in a semicircle around the teacher's; green writing boards and yellow chalk. But I longed for Newfound School, with its old desks bolted to the oil-soaked floor, and the huge oak tree in the yard, scarred with everyone's initials. I yearned for the good hours when the teacher taught the other side of the room and I read and heard the faraway chugging of the engine and the singing of the saw as it cut through timber at the sawmill down by the creek—or else, went to other classes and told stories.

J. D. Marler and his little brother Carl came back to school, and the scandal of the head lice, if not forgotten, was at least dropped. But Miss Hudspeth was relentless. The students from Newfound became her pet project. She had been a missionary in Central America, and I suppose we reminded her of the diseased, undernourished children she had known there. We shocked her with our ignorance, our backwardness, and our poverty in the midst of the splendor of West Madison. She disapproved of our sack lunches. "For only pennies a day, you can have a hot, nourishing meal," she would say. "Be sure to tell your fathers and mothers."

I never grew accustomed to feeling shame. Each time, it flared up hotter than before, and raced from the center out, popping and cracking like a brush fire, leaving everything black and smoldering inside.

When Miss Hudspeth brought just us students from Newfound together for a lecture, we at least enjoyed a kind of privacy in which to feel ashamed of ourselves. But usually we were scattered among the others, especially when she showed films in the darkened gym. One of these films was called "The Wheel of Good Health," and showed healthy, happy children eating fresh fruits, green leafy vegetables, yellow vegetables, cheese, milk, fish, poultry, and all the rest, maintaining all the while, in spite of the constant chewing, expressions of pure delight. A recurring picture of a wheel showed the basic seven daily requirements for good nutrition.

When the film ended, Miss Hudspeth motioned for the lights to be turned on, stood out on the gym floor with her hands clasped together, and talked to us about our personal diets. She asked several students what they had had for breakfast that morning, and they recited: bacon, eggs, toast, milk, cereal—all the lovely, approved things.

"What about you little Newfound folk?" she asked, pointing to my brother Eugene, who was sitting on the front row of bleachers looking up at her. Eugene always listened as if his life depended on it, but he never realized how backward he was. "You, little brown-eyes," Miss Hudspeth said, "what did you eat for breakfast?"

Eugene started rocking back and forth nervously, and gripped his jeans at the knees. "Biscuits," he said, his voice sounding unusually high and thin in the gym; ". . . and sawmill gravy," he continued, in the singsong of recitation. I could see Miss Hudspeth was shocked, as no doubt she knew she would be, for she smiled even more fiercely, and pointed to another child. But Eugene was not through reciting. ". . . and molasses," he intoned, "*new* molasses!"

A half-mad, hysterical laugh rose to the high ceiling of the gym and bounced back before I realized that it was I who had laughed. I cringed down, all crumbling ashes inside, and looked to see whether anyone on either side of me knew that Eugene was my brother.

⋙ 17 ⋘

D AD CAME FROM Mountain City one Saturday to take Jeanette, Eugene, and me down to Grandma and Grandpa Wells's. He drove up in a blue Buick—he had a different car every month or two—and walked into the yard under the big maple tree, kicking up the big yellow leaves that had fallen. Eugene, Jeanette, and I came out to meet him. Dad picked up Jeanette and lifted her high. Eugene walked over and ran his hand over the hood of the blue Buick.

Mom came out on the porch. She told Dad she wished he'd come on Sunday, the way he usually did, because she'd wanted us kids to help pick up the potatoes Grandpa Smith was going to plow out today.

Dad said he couldn't get help at the boat dock for Sunday, but he did have somebody to help out today.

"Boat dock?" Mom said. She'd thought he was running a miniature golf course in Mountain City.

Dad said he was, but that business dropped off in the

fall. He was in on this marina, this boat dock on Big Ivy Lake, and the fall fishing was in full swing.

Mom thought it was a trout pond he had.

He was out of that. Now he was in on this marina. He might start making fiberglass boats, too, and boat trailers.

It was all very confusing.

Mom sniffed. There was a long silence.

Dad stood looking down, making a little pile of maple leaves with his right foot while Jeanette pulled his left arm, almost tipping him over. Dad said he guessed he could come another time.

"No!" Jeanette said.

Well, no, Mom said. She just wished he'd send word if he was coming other than on Sunday.

Dad said he didn't always know far enough ahead to send word.

"Go on with your Daddy," Mom said to us.

Dad said he might have us back in time for us to help pick up the potatoes. "You got the check?" he asked Mom over his shoulder as we headed to the blue Buick.

Mom said she did. She stood on the porch watching us turn and then went back into the house.

Eugene had run ahead and got in the front seat beside Dad. Jeanette and I sat in the back seat. "I'd rather go to Grandpa Wells's store," Eugene said. "We can walk to Grandpa and Grandma Wells's anytime we want to, but only Robert gets to go as far as the store."

"Yeah," Jeanette said. "I want to go to the store, and I want to go to Grandma and Grandpa Wells's, *too*!"

Dad said we could drive down to the store first. Then we'd come back to Grandma and Grandpa Wells's. Eugene sat close beside Dad and helped him steer, but Dad never took his hand off the steering wheel, either. When we got out of the car at the store and started in, Jeanette pulled Dad off toward the gas pumps and he bent down as she whispered something in his ear. He nodded.

˙ "I bet she's askin' for somethin'," Eugene said to Dad. "If she gets to buy somethin', we do too."

"She wasn't asking for anything for herself," Dad said. "Were you, Sis?"

Jeanette shook her head.

"She wants to get Grandpa Wells something for his birthday."

Jeanette liked to give parties. She used to give parties for her pinecone dolls, and wrap little gifts for them, and she never let a birthday go by in the family without having a party and giving gifts. She liked a birthday party for somebody else as much as she liked one on her own birthday. Maybe more. Jeanette knew all our birthdays—Mom's, Dad's, Eugene's, mine, Grandma and Grandpa Smith's, Grandma and Grandpa Wells's. If we didn't know what to get for someone's birthday, she'd tell us what they ought to get from us. Mostly she made the gifts she gave, and drew the cards, but she also saved up money she got from Mom or Dad, or Grandma or Grandpa Smith, and she'd buy gifts for our birthdays—a kerchief for Grandma Smith, a manicure set for Mom, a comic book for Eugene.

For Grandpa Wells's birthday, which wasn't until the following Wednesday, Jeanette had enough money to get him either a handkerchief or a pair of socks, but she couldn't decide which she should get. Dad said he would buy the socks if she would buy the handkerchief, and the socks could be from him. Well, then, Jeanette said, Robert and Eugene ought to get him something, too, and Mom. And what about Grandma and Grandpa Smith?

Dad said the big people could get their own gifts, but Eugene and I could get Grandpa Wells something and he would pay for it. Eugene chose green after-shave lotion, and I picked out a package of Model pipe tobacco, because I knew that was the brand he smoked. I liked to watch the neat way he could hold his pipe in his one hand and tamp the tobacco in with his finger at the same time.

Then Jeanette had to have wrapping paper, for she wanted to wrap the gifts right away. At first Grady Plemmons, his black price marker behind his ear, said he didn't have any gift-wrapping paper in the store, but then he found some, only it was for Christmas, red and green with silver bells and stars and angels, but Jeanette said that was all right. So Jeanette paid for the handkerchief and Dad paid for everything else, including wrapping paper, scotch tape, and some To/From cards.

Jeanette wrapped the gifts there in the store, borrowing Grady's scissors to cut the wrapping paper to the right size for each gift, using his price marker to fill out the cards.

I got in the front seat with Dad when we left the store, but I didn't ask to steer. Eugene had to get in the back seat with Jeanette. She sat holding the birthday gifts in her lap, but she didn't bring them in the house when we got there. Sometime that afternoon, she told us later, she'd sneaked back out to the car and brought the gifts into the house and hidden them in the back bedroom that no one ever went into. That way, she explained, the birthday party would be a surprise. We'd come over next Wednesday after school, and we wouldn't have any gifts, so Grandpa Wells would think, "Well, I don't see any gifts, and it's too late, anyway, so I guess I won't get a birthday party." Then she'd get the gifts out of the back bedroom and we'd all say, "Surprise, Grandpa! Happy birthday!" and then Grandma Wells could set out some cake or some muffins—she always had cake or muffins—and we could have some milk, and Grandpa Wells could have coffee with his cake or muffin, because he always drank coffee. We ought to have candles, but we couldn't possibly have enough candles for all the years Grandpa Wells was. Maybe we could have just one candle on Grandpa Wells's muffin. She knew where there were some little candles in a drawer up at Grandma and Grandpa Smith's, left over from Eugene's birthday.

Dad got us back to Grandma and Grandpa Smith's by mid-afternoon and drove on back to Mountain City. By that time Grandpa Smith had plowed up the whole potato patch. You could look down the rows and see the potatoes turned up in the warm afternoon sun. Grandma and Grandpa Smith and Mom were out in the patch gathering potatoes. Mom got us each a basket and set us to helping.

Working in the row beside me, Jeanette started to worry that Grandma Wells might not have any cake or muffins when we went down there on Wednesday for the birthday party. Maybe we ought to make a cake and take it down there with us, just to make sure we had one. We could hide it in the rosebushes and go in first, and *then* go out a few minutes later and bring it in.

"You're missin' a lot of 'em," Eugene told Jeanette. "You can't always see 'em. You have to stir the dirt around." He reached over into Jeanette's row, raked through the loose dirt with his hand, and turned up a big, fat potato. "Look!" he said. Then he uncovered another. "Look!"

But Jeanette was preoccupied with Grandpa Wells's birthday party. When she tried to get Grandma Smith to help her bake a cake, Grandma Smith said, "Why, there's half a cake right there in the pie safe."

Mom heard them talking about cake, thought Jeanette was wanting to eat cake before supper, and said Jeanette couldn't have any.

Jeanette said she meant a cake for Wednesday.

"She's not finding nearly all of 'em!" Eugene said. Exasperated with Jeanette, he uncovered another potato she had missed. "Somebody might as well just do her row over!"

Grandma Smith said she didn't know what Jeanette was talking about—a cake for Wednesday? So Jeanette explained the whole thing: how next Wednesday was Grandpa Wells's birthday and we had already got him some gifts and hidden them in the house and we were going to go over there and surprise him.

Grandma Smith's right hand went up to the side of her weathered face, the way it always did when she was surprised.

Mom looked dubious at first. But it turned out she thought Jeanette was talking about a birthday cake for Grandma Wells. When she understood Jeanette wanted to bake a cake for Grandpa Wells, not Grandma Wells, she said that would be all right.

Mom, Jeanette, and Grandma Smith went to the house to start supper, leaving Eugene, Grandpa Smith, and me to hole up the potatoes for the winter. We knew how to do it, for we'd helped do it last fall, too. Grandpa Smith said we had so many potatoes this year, we'd have to do two potato holes, so we dug two shallow depressions in the ground at the edge of the potato patch. We carried the baskets of potatoes and gently dumped them into the two depressions, piling them up until there were two cone-shaped mounds. We covered the mounds with straw from the barn loft, then, working with shovels, tossed dirt on the straw mounds. At the bottom of each mound Grandpa Smith placed a short length of stovepipe that extended beyond the dirt, but back through the straw to the potatoes. Finishing up, we stuffed the stovepipes tight with straw. Now when the cold weather came and we needed potatoes, we could remove the straw, reach into the pipe, and pull the potatoes out, one or two at a time. And as we used them up, others would roll down into their place.

At supper Jeanette couldn't wait to start baking the birthday cake. "You said we could," she reminded Mom.

But Mom thought it was too late to start baking a cake, and Grandma Smith agreed.

What about tomorrow?

Tomorrow was Sunday, a day of rest, Mom said.

Jeanette didn't say anything more about the cake. But she hadn't given up. After supper she said, "Well, Monday! Monday is still a long time before Wednesday."

"Well, maybe," Mom said.

"Well, for sure!" Jeanette got Mom's hairbrush and started brushing Mom's hair, something she knew Mom liked her to do. "Say 'Well, for sure.' "

"Well . . ." Mom said.

"You say 'Well, for sure,' too, Grandma!"

"Well . . ." Grandma Smith said.

➤➤➤ ◄◄◄

JEANETTE AND GRANDMA SMITH baked the cake on Monday, after we got home from school, and it was already iced and in the pie safe by the time Mom got home from Jewell Hill. Jeanette led Mom by the hand to the pie safe and opened one of the doors that had tin panels with nail holes punched in the shape of a star. Jeanette wrote a note that said "Do not touch," and stood it on the shelf in front of the cake.

On Tuesday when Mom came home, Jeanette led Mom to the pie safe and showed her the cake again.

"You already showed it to her once," Eugene said. "How many times are you going to show it to her?"

"As many as I want to!" Jeanette said. "I'm just showing her nobody's cut a piece from it yet."

"I might still yet," Eugene said.

"You do and you'll get the thrashing of your life," Jeanette said.

If he got a thrashing, it wouldn't be from Jeanette, Eugene allowed.

Mom told Eugene and Jeanette to hush.

After supper Jeanette got out her school scissors and colored pencils and made Grandpa Wells a birthday card. She didn't like it, though, so she tore it up and started working on another one.

On Wednesday when we got home from school, everything was ready. Jeanette gave me a candle and told me to keep it in my shirt pocket. She carried the cake on one of Grandma Smith's biggest plates, covered with a clean white cloth. Eugene didn't have to carry anything. We walked down out of the holler and followed the old wagon road around the hill, the way we always went when we walked down to Grandma and Grandpa Wells's. We were like the three wise men bringing gifts in the Christmas story, I thought.

Jeanette got tired carrying the cake and asked me to carry it a while—but I'd better not drop it. I carried the cake a while, and when Jeanette's arms were rested, she carried it again. We walked on, switching the cake back and forth between us. Each time we switched, Jeanette carried the cake a shorter distance, and I carried it farther.

When we came around the hill and looked down toward Grandma and Grandpa Wells's big white house, Eugene said, "Somebody's there."

"Then they can just come to the party, too," Jeanette said.

"It's a van," Eugene said. "Look, what a van!"

As we got closer, we could see that the van was painted all sorts of carnival colors—red, yellow, purple, and there were dragon faces, clouds, crags, and waterfalls painted on it. When we got to the edge of the yard, where Jeanette hid the cake under the rosebushes, I saw that the van had California license plates. We peered inside it. There was a lot of trash on the floor, and the ashtray overflowed with cigarette butts that had lipstick on them. There was a guitar case in the back, along with magazines, newspapers, and clothes scattered everywhere.

We found out from Grandma Wells that Grandpa Wells had gone to the sawmill but would be back later. And the colorful van was in the drive because Aunt Alma had come home unexpectedly—Aunt Alma who had a career in the theater. Only she was in television now, and was traveling from California to Nashville, Tennessee, with, well, with a friend, another person in theater and television, and they had arrived earlier in the afternoon, exhausted, and they were resting now.

California is on the West Coast, Grandma Wells said. Its capital is Sacramento. Nashville is Tennessee's capital, she said. Then she took us in the parlor and got out an atlas and showed us California and Tennessee on a map of the United States. She asked if we studied geography in school. We said we did. She talked a long time about New Orleans and a trip she and Grandpa Wells had taken there once. While she was telling about the trip, Jeanette sneaked away, but Grandma Wells didn't notice. Grandma Wells was still showing us places on the map when Jeanette came back in and whispered in my ear. She wanted me to come outside.

It was a while before Grandma Wells finished—she seemed more talkative than usual—and Jeanette kept pulling on my arm. Finally she said she wanted to show me something in the yard. "Don't play around that car," Grandma Wells said. I followed Jeanette outside. We went all the way out to the rosebushes where the cake was hidden before Jeanette turned and, on the edge of tears, said Aunt Alma was asleep in the room where Grandpa Wells's birthday gifts were hidden.

"Did you see Aunt Alma?" I asked.

"No, I just went to the door and opened it a little and saw somebody was in the bed, so I closed it again."

"Are the gifts under the bed?" I asked her.

"No, they're in the bottom dresser drawer, under pillowcases."

I told Jeanette that if she would go back in and stay with Eugene and Grandma Wells, I would try to get the gifts out of the room.

"Can you?"

"I'll try," I said.

"But can you?" Jeanette insisted.

"I think I can sneak in without waking them up," I said. "Now, go on."

I went back in the house through a side door that opened onto the long porch, tiptoed along the hall, got down on my hands and knees, and gently pushed open the door of the back bedroom. I didn't hear anything. I could see the dresser on the far side of the room, and started crawling toward it on my hands and knees. I stopped and looked around. Clothes lay puddled on the floor. A shirt and pair of pants lay draped over a chair. A blond wig hung from a bedpost. On the nightstand stood a bottle of liquor, a big green bottle of Seven-Up, and some glasses. I could see that Aunt Alma lay on the far side of the bed, her face toward the wall. But the other sleeper's face was turned to me. It had long hair, too, like a woman, but also a mustache. And the arm that lay on top of the sheet was a man's.

I crawled on to the dresser, eased the bottom drawer open, and took the gifts out from under the pillowcases one at a time, being careful not to crackle the paper. My heart almost stopped beating when Aunt Alma rolled over against the wall, bumped it, and lay there making little smacking sounds with her lips. I waited until she was quiet again. There was no way to hold the gifts and crawl back to the door on my hands and knees, so I stacked the gifts carefully, with the flat bottle of shaving lotion on top, stood up, and tiptoed to the door. Once out of the room, I held the gifts in one hand and pulled the door to with the other.

Grandpa Wells drove up just as I was coming out of the rosebushes, where I'd hidden the gifts with the cake. We went in the house together. I whispered to Jeanette that I'd got the gifts, and she took over. She told Grandma and Grandpa Wells they had to sit right where they were and not move. Grandma Wells looked puzzled at first, but then she smiled. Grandpa Wells took off his glasses, rubbed his eyes with his thumb and middle finger, and put his glasses on again.

We went out, got the cake and gifts out of the rosebushes, and came in again, Jeanette carrying the cake, Eugene and I following with the gifts.

"Surprise, surprise!" Jeanette said. "Happy birthday, Grandpa Wells!"

➤➤➤ ⬅⬅⬅

JEANETTE WAS DISAPPOINTED that Aunt Alma and the other actress couldn't come to the party, too. She had never seen Aunt Alma "in real"—only her picture there on the mantelpiece. And she'd like to see the other actress, too. But Grandma Wells said no, it wouldn't do to wake them, they had been so tired from the long drive, and still had a long trip ahead of them.

Otherwise, Jeanette was pleased with the party. Grandpa Wells was completely surprised, and he liked the gifts we'd bought in his own store. "You walked up on my blind side that time," he admitted. Jeanette told about buying the gifts on Saturday, making the cake, and hiding it in the rosebush. But she didn't tell how I'd had to slip into the back bedroom where Aunt Alma was sleeping and get the gifts.

"Did you see them?" Jeanette asked me when we were walking back up the holler to Grandma and Grandpa Smith's after the party.

"The shades were pulled down, it was pretty dark, and they were all covered up, mostly," I said. Which was true, mostly.

"I wanted to see Aunt Alma in real," Jeanette said. "She's pretty in her picture. I'll bet she's pretty in real, too."

"She wears a wig," I told Jeanette. "It was hanging on the bedpost, like a coonskin cap."

Jeanette wanted to know what color Aunt Alma's real hair was. I said I thought it was black, like Dad's.

Maybe it was the other actress's wig, Jeanette said. I said I didn't think so.

Eugene said he wished he had him a van like Aunt Alma's, with swirly colors and dragon faces on it.

Jeanette insisted that we go back down to Grandma and Grandpa Wells's the next afternoon, for she hoped Aunt Alma and the other actress would still be there. But they had left a little before noon while we were still in school, Grandma Wells said, headed for Nashville. She gave us some of the cake left over from Grandpa Wells's birthday party, and we walked back up the holler. Jeanette walked slowly and mumbled to herself, still frustrated and disappointed over not getting to see Aunt Alma and the other actress. Eugene picked up rocks and threw them at fenceposts.

I walked with a new knowledge—that words had little side doors and back entrances, and sometimes words crept silently on hands and knees. Words concealed surprises, the way the rosebushes hid a birthday cake; the way the back bedroom kept Grandpa Wells's surprise, and one for me as well. Words sometimes babbled about states and capitals, I knew, but they weren't always good maps. And sometimes words kept silent when they could have spoken.

⇛ 18 ⇚

As our second christmas at Grandma and Grandpa Smith's drew near, Jeanette kept asking when we could put up a tree.

Already, with Grandma Smith's help, she had found some holly, and Eugene had climbed the big oak tree above the barn and fetched down sprigs of mistletoe. "Whose toe will never be stubbed or pinched?" Jeanette asked, and then answered her own question. "Mistletoe's! Grandpa said!" Now she was making decorations—stringing popcorn on sewing thread, making paper chains with glue and art paper.

Grandma and Mom talked her into a small tree, for they had set up quilting frames in the living room and worked on quilts in the evening. Eugene said he knew where lots of good Christmas trees were. Mom sent me with Eugene and Jeanette, to make sure they didn't get a tree that was too big. Standing in her coat and kerchief, like a little Grandma Smith, Jeanette considered several trees and finally decided on the biggest one I thought Mom would let us bring in the house. Eugene sawed it off at the ground with Grandpa's bucksaw, and we dragged it home.

That evening, the first day of our Christmas vacation, we all had something to do. Grandma Smith and Mom quilted in the living room. Jeanette decorated the tree. Grandpa Smith sat making twists of red tobacco to hang in the corner of the kitchen by the red peppers Grandma had strung there. In the kitchen I took turns with Eugene working the dasher up and down in the wooden churn. When it wasn't my turn, I read in my poetry book and ate popcorn from the big bowlful Jeanette had popped.

Jeanette had learned all of Grandma Smith's rhymes and riddles and said them at every opportunity. "What's big at the bottom, little at the top, thing in the middle goes flippety-flop?" she asked.

"Your mouth," Eugene said from the kitchen.

"No, a churn!" Jeanette said. "You're churning right now and you couldn't even guess!"

"I know one you can't get," Eugene said. "Dad gave it to you, but it was Grandpa Wells's. But Grandpa Wells kept it, but you use it, too. And I do, too."

Jeanette studied. "Does Robert use it?"

"Yeah, he uses it, too," Eugene said.

Jeanette couldn't figure the answer. Eugene said that proved she wasn't as smart as she thought she was.

Jeanette said it was a dumb riddle, anyway, and changed the subject. She wanted Grandma Smith to tell about Christmas in the olden days.

Christmas was a lot different when she was a little girl, Grandma Smith said. You didn't hear so much about Santa Claus. Now it's all mostly Santa Claus. Grandma Smith believed in Old Christmas, which was January 6. The twelve days from Christmas Day to January 6 were the twelve days of Christmas.

Mom sat opposite Grandma Smith at the quilting frame, a thimble on her middle finger. Mom said she believed in Old Christmas, too. And she believed that on Christmas Eve cattle kneeled down, just as they had when Baby Jesus was born.

"In our barn, too?" Jeanette said, turning from the half-decorated tree. "Sarah and Betsy—will they kneel down on Christmas Eve?"

"I've always heard it," Grandma said.

"What about Bertie?" Jeanette asked Grandpa Smith. "Do mules kneel down on Christmas Eve, Grandpa?"

Grandpa Smith didn't hear Jeanette. I told him what she'd said.

"If cows can, Bertie can," Grandpa Smith said, and gave me a knowing look.

"Bertie can open the latch on her stall door with her nose," Eugene said.

Jeanette quickly whispered something into Grandma Smith's ear and Grandma Smith whispered something back. Looking triumphant, she went back to cutting a star out of cardboard. "Eugene, is it my name?" she half-sang.

"Is what your name?" Eugene asked.

"Is it my name that Daddy gave me, but Grandpa Wells kept, but I use, and you use, and Robert, too?"

Eugene said he knew one of us must have told Jeanette the answer, but we played dumb.

Jeanette covered the cardboard star with foil, stood on a chair, and fastened it to the top of the Christmas tree.

᠉19᠊

WHEN DAD WOULD COME and take us down to
Grandma and Grandpa Wells's, he'd talk to
Grandpa Wells about businesses they could
get into. While Eugene and Jeanette prowled upstairs, the
way I used to, or played outside, I'd sit and listen as Dad
tried to interest Grandpa Wells in starting a worm farm.
They could sell the worms in bait shops around Big Ivy
Lake, or to tourists who fished the put-and-take trout ponds.
Or they could raise rabbits right there on the farm—goats,
too. They could raise Christmas trees. He tried to interest
Grandpa Wells in investing in storage buildings in Mountain City. Dad had lots of ideas for businesses, but he
needed money from Grandpa Wells to get started in them.

Grandpa Wells couldn't see how any of Dad's ideas would
turn a profit. It might be possible to make money on Christmas trees, eventually, but that was a long-term proposition.

A few weeks later, when he came to take us down to
Grandpa Wells's, Dad was pulling a trailer behind his car,

and standing in the trailer was a big plastic Indian, about twelve feet tall, with a feather in his hair. For the whole time we visited with Grandma and Grandpa Wells, the Indian stood in the trailer, holding up his hand as if he were saying "How!" Dad explained to Grandpa Wells that the Indian was a sign; he was selling the sign to a fireworks store that was opening up at the state line. The store was going to be called "Indian Joe's."

"Honestly, James!" Grandma Wells said. "How do you get involved in these schemes?" She went to the window and looked out at the plastic Indian standing in the trailer.

Dad said the legislature had changed the fireworks law, and these fireworks stands were going up all along the state line. He said Grandpa Wells ought to lease some land over there along the line somewhere and throw up three or four stands. Dad would run them for him.

Grandma Wells spoke for Grandpa; she said he wasn't going to build fireworks stands.

Grandpa Wells took his glasses off with his one hand, set them down on the table, rubbed the bridge of his nose, and put them back on again.

Grandma Wells looked over at me. "Robert, go see what your brother and sister are doing," she said.

I climbed the stairs knowing Grandma Wells was sending me away because she was going to say something she didn't want me to hear. I clomped heavily in the upstairs hall. Jeanette was trying on old hats in the first bedroom on the left. At the end of the hall Eugene had picked up the big whorled seashell used for a doorstop and was holding it to his ear. I then crept back to the top of the stairs to listen. Sure enough, Grandma Wells was giving Dad a lecture. I couldn't hear everything, but I heard her mention child support, custody, "this divorce," "irreconcilable differences," "final decree."

I slipped quietly down the stairs and back into the parlor just as Grandma Wells was telling Dad he should find a line of work and stay with it instead of flitting from one thing to the next. She looked up at me.

"They're just playing," I said.

There was a silence.

Grandpa Wells cleared his throat. He told Dad that what his mama said made a lot of sense. Dad ought to think about it.

That very evening, back at Grandma and Grandpa Smith's, I asked Mom about the divorce. I told her I had heard Grandma Wells talking about it.

"What did she say?" Mom asked.

"I just heard her talk about it to Dad. I was upstairs and didn't hear it all."

Mom said the divorce would be in about two months. She and Dad had to be separated a certain length of time before the divorce could take place, and the time was about up.

The word made my breath tighter and somehow made me think of funerals, Bible verses, and Sunday morning radio sermons broadcast from echoing churches. It was a dark word, like a thundercloud. It was a word like "salvation" or "judgment." What would happen when the separation became divorce? I wanted to ask something but I wasn't sure what. I knew what separation was, and I figured divorce must be worse. Finally, I asked: "Couldn't you just stay separated and not get divorced?"

No, Mom said, you got divorced after the period of separation was up.

Did divorce mean we wouldn't be allowed to see Dad anymore? I held my breath.

Why, no, Mom said. We'd get to see Dad just the same as before.

I was relieved. I said I was going to tell Eugene and Jeanette.

"Is that what they think?" Mom asked.

I said I didn't know, but I wanted to tell them. I think I wanted to tell Eugene and Jeanette just to reassure myself.

But instead of letting me tell them, Mom sent me to bring Eugene and Jeanette into her room, where she sat us down and explained the whole thing. Two or three times she said Dad would still be coming to see us, just like he had been doing. Did Jeanette understand? Yes. Did Eugene? Um-hum. Robert? Yes.

I believed her, but I wasn't really reassured until Dad came for us the following Sunday. He was still pulling the trailer behind his car, and this time he had a shiny black plastic bull, about eight feet tall, in the trailer. The bull was another sign for a fireworks stand.

Grandma Wells shook her head when she saw it. She asked Dad if he had given any more thought to what she'd said about finding a line of work and staying with it.

"Nowadays," Dad said, "you can have one job in a lot of places, or a lot of jobs in one place."

Grandma Wells said she didn't believe that. She'd been thinking about a suitable line of work for Dad, and had even made an inquiry on Dad's behalf to Congressman Hatcher.

Grandpa Wells looked at Dad. "Old Wilbur Hatcher. I should have thought of him myself. All I'm always doing for him in Madison. Get in touch with Wilbur," Grandpa Wells advised. "I just bet he can scare you up something."

Grandma Wells was pleased when Dad took her advice. Through Congressman Hatcher he got a job that summer measuring tobacco allotments in Madison County, while he still had an interest in the boat dock and marina on Big Ivy Lake. She was really pleased when, after that, Dad became Congressman Hatcher's assistant, with an office in Mountain City. She spoke of Dad's "position" and thought the job more in keeping with Dad's background and abilities. After all, Dad had been to college, and his great-uncle Robert had been a judge and later mayor of Jewell Hill. Dad was suited to a political position, she said.

Suited. I wondered if that was why Dad wore a suit when he came for us now. He told Mom about his new job. She said she hoped it worked out for him, and then talked about her new job at Blue Ridge Manufacturing, the one she got after she'd learned to type.

Working for Walter Lee Rogers, was it? Dad wanted to know.

Yes, Mom said. And now she was learning bookkeeping, too.

Later I heard Mom telling Grandma Smith about Dad's new job. "Gone into politics," she said. She reckoned that might be all right for Dad. It sure wouldn't suit her. Which was probably one of the reasons they had never been able to get along, though it had taken her a long time to realize it.

Mom wore a new black suit, with her hair coiled and held tight with combs, when she went to Mountain City for the final divorce decree. All that mid-June morning and afternoon, about a week after I'd finished eighth grade, I looked and listened, alert for any difference the divorce would bring. I couldn't detect any. Bertie stood with her head down in the pasture. Sarah and Betsy grazed. Grandpa Smith's old Dominecker rooster crowed and strutted. On the ridge above the barn a woodpecker hammered on a hollow tree. And the mountains, their slopes dappled with sun and shadow, stood serene and unconcerned all around Grandma and Grandpa Smith's house.

Dad came for us, sometimes on Saturday, but usually on Sunday, just as he had before. But in his new job—and always in a suit now—he was different. He used words like "caucus" and "predecessor." He talked about roads and dams with Grandma and Grandpa Wells, about strip-mine regulations in Congressman Hatcher's district, and a fish fry he was organizing for local political leaders.

⇛ 20 ⇚

IN THE ROW beside me Eugene bent down a tall stalk of tobacco and stood reaching up with his skinny brown arms. "Wished it'd storm," he said. "We wouldn't have to sucker this tobacco if it stormed."

Eugene was a lot shorter than I was. He had to bend down the tall stalks of tobacco to reach the suckers in the top.

"It's hot enough," I said. "Maybe it'll come a storm."

"If we didn't have to sucker this tobacco, we could go to the creek—and swing, and cool off."

"J. D. Marler and that bunch—they've probably already torn down that grapevine by now," I said. I had half a mind to tear it down myself, if they hadn't. I couldn't fish that big pond in the creek with Eugene swinging out over it on that grapevine.

"Grandpa takes too much pains," Eugene grumbled. "He just makes work for us. And Coy Marler—he suckers his tobacco early, when it's cool."

"You could ask Grandpa," I said. "If you want to go to

the creek, why don't you just ask him?" I was dying to go to the creek myself, but I knew it would be better if Eugene asked Grandpa. Eugene had been sick a lot all spring, and he was puny, and tired out easily. Sometimes, when Eugene looked peaked, Grandpa took pity on him and I got out of work, too.

"I believe I will ask him," Eugene said. "I'll tell him I'm tired. I am pretty tired."

We were almost to the end of the field. My mouth was so dry I could spit cotton. Down between the rows of tobacco no air stirred. My shirt was wet and sticking to my back; I had tobacco gum on my arms and ears and in my hair. Sweat tickled my eyebrows and crept into the corners of my eyes and stung.

I finished my row ahead of Eugene. Crumbling a clod in my hands to rub off the tobacco gum, I sat down beside the water jar. It was spring water, so cold it hurt when it hit the bottom of my stomach. I screwed the cap back on the jar and lay with my head under a big tobacco leaf.

When he finished his row, Eugene came and drank. The rim of the jar made a red place on his nose. "Wish it'd storm," he said again.

It was hot enough to storm. The clouds back of Horse Knob were piled up on flat dark bottoms, fat and white, with curlicues, like big scoops of ice cream on plates.

Grandpa Smith saw us and came up from the branch bank, carrying his mowing blade on his shoulder.

"You reckon it'd do any good to ask him?" Eugene said.

"You'd better," I said, "if you want to go to the creek."

Grandpa Smith laid his mowing blade on the ground and grinned down at us. "That all you fellers do up here? Lay in the shade?" He squatted beside the water jar, took just a little water, swished it around in his mouth, and spat half of it out. He could work all day on just a swallow of water, and he didn't sweat. I drank too much water, and now the sweat was oozing out all over me. Grandpa Smith was dry. His face looked looked just a little oily, like rich pine.

I could tell by the way Eugene was biting his fingernails that he was getting ready to ask Grandpa if we could go to the creek. He made a half-moon in the dirt with his heel and said, "Grandpa, I don't see any need to sucker this tobacco anymore. It's got its spread. So high now I have to take and bend it over to reach in the top."

"You're not breakin' it, I hope," Grandpa said.

"No, I just take and bend the stalk over a little. It tires my arms out."

Grandpa Smith said he wished he had another half-acre of tobacco as good as this patch. He'd build another barn to house it.

"I'm gonna get me another pair of jeans," Eugene said. "This old measurin' worm's measuring me for a pair."

Eugene's mind was wandering. I nudged him and jerked my head toward Grandpa Smith. But Eugene had lost his nerve. He wouldn't ask if we could go to the creek.

Taking a whetstone out of his back pocket, Grandpa Smith gave the mowing blade a few licks and turned back to the branch bank.

"Why didn't you ask him?" I said to Eugene. We took two more rows and started back through the field.

"I did ask him—sort of."

"Yeah, sort of. Then you started talkin' about a measuring worm!"

We didn't talk till we'd suckered through our rows and

sat down to rest again. Eugene said he wasn't doing a good job. He was getting suckers on the bottoms of the stalks until his back got tired, then the suckers up high until his arms got tired.

I had been skipping, too, but I didn't tell Eugene.

He walked up the edge of the field, counting the rows we had to finish. "Twenty dad-burn rows!" he said. He stood twisting his heel in the dirt. "We could finish after we milked—after supper. What difference does it make, as long as we finish sometime?"

I was ready to go to the creek, but I didn't let on. "We might as well finish," I said. "I couldn't fish, anyway, with you swinging out over the hole, makin' a shadow."

Eugene picked up three rocks from a pile at the edge of the field and laid them beside the row where we had stopped suckering. "You can fish first. I won't want to swing till you get through fishin'."

"You'll have to keep still," I told him, as he followed me along the edge of the field.

We crawled under the fence and walked through the pasture, kicking up grasshoppers in front of us. We each caught a handful of grasshoppers for fishbait. Eugene found an old Prince Albert can to put them in. A cloud shadow skimmed over the pasture. I aimed to pick up my fishing pole at the Hollow Rock, where I had it hidden. When we got there, I crawled back under the rock to get my pole. It was gone.

"Them Marlers," Eugene said. "They may be down at the creek, fishin' with your pole. Hope they are. We'll chug rocks in the hole."

"I'll chug one at the side of J. D. Marler's head if he's got my pole again," I said.

We sneaked down to the creek, hoping to catch J. D. But nobody was there.

"Least they didn't tear down the grapevine," Eugene said.

"You wait a minute," I said. "You said I could fish before we swung." I thought I might find one of the Marlers' throwlines. I looked around. Bees on the sandbar sucked water out of damp sand. I looked from one end of the sandbar to the other, but I couldn't find a throwline. "Let's go in," I said to Eugene.

"We can't. Grandpa'll know we've been down here if we get our heads wet. So we might as well swing." Eugene grabbed hold of the vine, took a little run, and swung off the rock out over the pond. When he came back, I gave him a push and sent him further out, almost to the honeysuckle on the far bank. Eugene's arms were so skinny, the little knots of muscle on them like hard, half-grown peaches. I didn't see how he held on. And he kept his feet drawn up under him, like an old hen when she flies up to roost.

"Why don't you let your feet hang down?" I said.

"I don't know why I keep scroochin' them up. I can't help it."

"I bet I get that J. D. Marler," I said. "Next time I'm down at his house, I'll look under the porch, where they keep their fishin' poles. I'll know my pole if I see it."

I crawled out to the edge of the rock and lay on my stomach looking down. I didn't care about the fishing pole, not really. The pond was a good place to come, even if I didn't get to fish. When I watched Eugene's shadow swing slowly back and forth on the still water, and heard the dull, lulling roar of the water coming down over rocks upstream, where the old spruce leaned halfway out over the creek, my thoughts stood still, like a leaf on the water, and it was as if every time I came to the pond was the same. I remembered steaming mornings when the honeysuckle on the far bank was alive with droning bees and screaming catbirds. The Marlers had corn in the bottom and Coy Marler plowed it, passing along behind the honeysuckle saying, "Gee . . . haw . . . Haw-w-w," and Eugene swung on the grapevine, then just as now. And lying in bed at night hearing the creek running, and turning my pillow over and lying with my face on the cool side and listening to the bird Grandpa Smith said was a nighthawk . . .

Eugene dragged his feet on the rock, rested, and swung again. Back and forth the vine swung, a black line on the water with a scrooched-up ball on the end, like a clock pendulum. A breeze sprang up. I turned over on my back, closed my eyes, and let the breeze blow over my face. I sat up. A shadow had come over the sandbar. A breeze rippled the water below the rock.

Again Eugene dragged his feet on the rock and stopped. "Gonna come a storm—'lectric storm, too, I bet."

A few leaves blew down on the water. I couldn't see any bees on the sandbar now. The breeze came again, a hard puff. It blew a minute and stopped, then blew again. It came right up the creek, rippling the smooth stretch of water. My shirt had been wet with sweat; now it was cold, and chilled me.

"We'd better go back," Eugene said. "If it was to storm, and Grandpa was to call us, and us not in the field—"

The sky over Horse Knob was the bluish color of a new

horseshoe. The wind came stronger. It was a queer wind. It came in a puff, stopped, then came again. When it thundered, we started back.

When we got up the creek bank and into the bottom, the wind was really blowing. I noticed another curious thing about it: it blew every which way. It blew the grass one way, stopped, then blew it another direction. And it was a cold wind that made chill bumps on my arms.

On the hill treetops crashed together and churned about, turning up the white undersides of leaves. I saw crooked blue lightning flick down the sky back of the hill. Then thunder rumbled. We started running toward the woods. Eugene ran behind me. Puffing along, he said if we didn't get home, Grandpa Smith would find out we'd sneaked out of the field and gone to the creek. We were almost to the fence when lightning struck it, cracking like a pistol, crackling and dancing on the barbed wire. Then thunder shook the ground.

We didn't stop running. We just turned away from the fence and kept going through the bottom. It started to rain, but not the way it usually does. I heard the rain coming, roaring in the trees; then it hit us all at once, so cold it took my breath. It was too late to get to the house before Grandpa called. We were close to the Hollow Rock, so we headed for it.

Eugene ran on. "I'm goin' home!"

"Grandpa's already called for us by now!"

"I don't care, I'm goin'!"

Something hit me on the head, then on the elbow. It hurt both times. Eugene stopped. He felt his arm and looked up. It had hurt him, too. I saw it bounce on the ground. Hail. It was hitting me all over and hurting, like a whole handful of willow switches. I turned and ran to the Hollow Rock. Hail bounced on the ground like shelled corn. I dived under the rock and yelled for Eugene. I ran out again and hollered, but the hail peppered me so hard I had to go back under the rock. Eugene came crashing through the bushes holding both hands over his head, running sideways. He was panting and whining, but I couldn't hear what he was saying for the wind and the awful noise of the hail ripping down through green leaves. Then Eugene hollered, "Now we've played hob!"

While we were looking, the hail turned to rain. For a minute, the awful noised stopped. The rain came in a sheet and blew through the bushes. Thunder bumped and rumbled, like wagon wheels on a wooden bridge. Then the hail was ripping and tearing and bouncing again. Little pieces of green leaves blew out of the bushes. Eugene was sitting with his knees drawn up against his chin, rocking back and forth, shivering. Once more the hail stopped, and that queer wind blew first one way and then another. Then the hail came again, tearing at the green leaves and rattling on the dead leaves on the ground. It popped off the ground like hot grease out of a pan.

When the hail stopped that time, it didn't come again. Rain fell steadily. Eugene was still sitting humped up. "You ought not to've let me talk you into comin'," he said, his teeth chattering. "We ought not to've come. I wouldn't have come if you hadn't come with me." He shuddered. "I wouldn't have come if I'd thought it would ruin the tobacco."

I hadn't even thought of the tobacco! I scrambled from under the rock and started running in the rain. Eugene came behind me. "It's hit! I know it's hit!" he yelled. "It has to be!" He hollered all the way. "If I'd known it would ruin the tobacco—." He fell and came sliding past me, hands out in the mud. "Grandpa'll kill us, and—and I don't much care if he does!"

We crawled under the fence and ran on the cow path. As soon as we got around the side of the hill, we could see down on the tobacco field.

"It's hit!" Eugene said.

Even from where we stood, it was an awful sight—the tobacco all blown and broken and riddled. The white undersides of tobacco leaves showed all over the patch. It looked as if a bunch of cows had run through it.

We walked the rest of the way across the pasture. The rain was slacking. It thundered far off, like somebody scooting a chair across the floor in a room overhead. We walked along the upper side of the field, our shoes making sucking sounds in the mud. The little creek at the far end of the field was up; we heard it coming down over the rocks. I never felt so sad, seeing the tobacco all riddled, twisted, broken, and blown down. A lot of it lay in mud.

I saw Grandpa. He had been standing at the corner of the field, but I didn't see him until he moved toward us. Eugene whined like a pup.

Grandpa Smith's black hat was beaten down over his eyes. "Where'd you fellers get to?"

"Under the Hollow Rock," I said.

"Robert let me talk him into goin'!" Eugene blurted. "I wanted to go but he let me talk him into it! I'm more to blame than he is." Eugene ran down to the rocks he had put by the row where we had stopped suckering. "I marked the place. I know where . . . we . . . stopped."

Eugene must have noticed the queer look Grandpa gave

him, for his voice got weaker and weaker. Finally, he said, "Grandpa, you're wet."

Grandpa Smith's shirt and overalls were drenched and clinging to him. He looked little, like a plucked chicken.

Grandma Smith came along the edge of the field wearing a coat and kerchief. Jeanette followed her, also in a coat and kerchief. They made their way through the mud, heads down. When she got to us and asked us where we were during the storm, Eugene started all over again, stuttering and mumbling and telling how I had let him talk me into going to the creek. Somehow Eugene had got the notion that the hail came because we left the tobacco field. Grandpa told him to hush about it, it didn't make any difference now.

Grandma Smith asked Grandpa what he'd thought he could do by standing out in the storm. Grandpa paid her no attention. She looked over the field. I remembered how she'd helped us set the tobacco and hoe it twice, coming to the field with us in the morning and working with us until it was time to go back to the house and fix lunch.

The sky back of Horse Knob was yellowish now. Clouds were scattering and streaming out, like an old sweater unraveling. Grandpa pulled off one of the riddled leaves and spread it out in his hands. "Well, Kate, looks like we'll have all raggedy lugs this year—one grade of leaf all the way to the top of the stalk."

Mom got home from work about five. She got out of Carlene Cantrell's car and walked straight down toward the tobacco field and stood looking. We came out of the house and walked down and stood with her. About that time, Grandpa

Wells came down in his old blue farm truck. Grandpa Smith walked over and stood with Grandpa Wells. "What's the best thing to do?" he asked Grandpa Wells.

Grandpa Wells said he thought some of the tobacco could be saved.

·Grandpa Smith nodded. "I believe a man can prime it, just start in at the bottom, grade it as you go, and work up to the top. It may or may not rot, owin' to the weather. But a man's got too much in it not to try and save it."

Grandpa Wells agreed, and drove on over to Marlers' to survey the damage there.

Dad came a little before dark that evening. He'd heard the news about the terrible hailstorm, and he came whipping off the Newfound Creek road and up our drive in a shiny black Oldsmobile, bouncing along. The car was still rocking as he got out and walked over to Grandma Smith and me. Dad said he'd be working with a lot of farmers whose crops had been damaged by the hail, helping them to get federal disaster loans, but he'd come by to see us first. He broke the top off a tobacco plant and threw it down in disgust. I could see Grandpa Smith didn't like that.

Come another year, Dad said, he'd see to it that Grandpa Wells took out crop insurance.

Come another year, Grandpa Smith said, he might sprout wings and fly. It was this year he was thinking about.

Dad went to the house and talked with Mom a few minutes, then left. He said he was going to set up a field office down at the store and gather as much information about damage done to crops as he could. He still wasn't clear about how extensive the storm had been. He had a lot to do.

It wasn't until I remembered we still had to milk that I

missed Eugene. I left Grandpa Smith in the field and went looking for him. I had an idea where he'd be. When he misbehaved and Mom or Grandpa Smith punished him for it, he went to the barn loft, squirmed down in the hay like a setting hen, and pouted. I got our milk buckets, walked to the barn, and climbed the ladder to the loft. Eugene was on his nest, just as I thought he'd be.

"Grandpa said for me to find you and for us to milk," I said.

Eugene didn't move.

"He's not goin' to whip you—if that's what you're worried about."

"I wouldn't care much if he did. I wouldn't care much if he wore me out."

"You couldn't help it because it stormed. What good would it've done if we'd stayed in the field? It would still have hailed. Dad was here and you didn't even get to see him."

I could see Eugene was shivering.

"You're gonna be sick again."

"I am not."

"You're shiverin' like a leaf. You'll have to take your medicine again."

"No, I won't."

"I'll tell Mom you're shiverin', and you'll have to take it—if you don't come on down."

Eugene crawled out of the hay. "You'd better not tell, because I'm not sick." He reached in his pocket and pulled out the Prince Albert can. "You want to save these hoppers?"

"No. Turn them loose and come on. We've got to milk."

Eugene started down the ladder. "I doubt if the cows'll give their milk down, they'll be so tore up."

"You're talkin' crazy," I said. "The cows don't know hail ruined our tobacco. And if they did know it, cows wouldn't care."

At supper Eugene was still shivering, but he got through without being noticed. If it had been any other time, Mom would have suspected something was wrong with him when he lay down after supper. But she was all torn up about the ruined tobacco crop, too, and trying to comfort Grandma and Grandpa Smith, telling them everything was going to be all right. Later, when I came to bed and lay beside Eugene, I felt him shivering.

"I told you you'd be sick, Eugene. You might as well tell and get it over with."

But he wouldn't tell, and begged me not to. He despised the medicine he'd have to take. Finally, he went to sleep. If I slept, it wasn't for long. Eugene rolled and mumbled and tore at the cover. He finally got so bad, hollering and moaning and talking in his sleep, Mom heard him and came in without my having to call her.

"Eugene? Eugene? Wake up! What's wrong with you?"

"The spring's runnin', make it stop!"

"What?"

Eugene sat up and rubbed his eyes.

Mom brought the medicine and a big spoon. Eugene crawled out of bed and tried to get behind the chest of drawers. She told me to hold Eugene and while I did, she poured the thick cherry-colored syrup out of the bottle into a big spoon. "Eugene, open!"

Eugene's teeth clicked on the spoon. He shuddered and pulled away from me.

"Wait!" Mom said to me. "He's not swallowed that yet. Don't you spit that out, you pup!"

Eugene swallowed, stretching his neck.

"Now, one more time," Mom said. "It's two spoonfuls."

Eugene bit the spoon.

"Swallow!"

He did and got back into bed. Mom sat by him and laid her hand on his forehead. For a long time, I thought Eugene was asleep; then he said, without opening his eyes, "Are we gonna start primin' tobacco tomorrow?"

"You go to sleep," Mom said. "We'll see about that tomorrow."

I kept turning my pillow over and lying with my face against the cool side, trying to sleep. But I couldn't, and neither could Grandpa Smith. I heard him on the back porch, rattling the dipper against the water bucket, and walking back and forth on the porch, making the boards creak. I got out of bed and sat in the dark by the open window with my blanket around me. I sat there the longest time, thinking something was wrong. Then I realized: the nighthawk that always sang down by the branch, its voice something hard and shiny in the dark, wasn't singing tonight. I smelled the bruised, beaten green tobacco in the cool air, and heard the creek, out of its banks, rushing and roaring and gurgling in the rocks louder than I had ever heard it before.

⋙ 21 ⋘

FALL CAME, and we started to school again. I entered
the ninth grade, Eugene seventh, Jeanette fifth. In
the afternoons when we came home from school,
and before we did chores, Eugene, Jeanette, and I picked
chinquapins on the ridges above Grandma and Grandpa
Smith's. We ate chinquapins, cracking the soft black hulls
with our teeth, then turning the nut out of the hull with
our tongues, until the tips of our tongues were sore. Jeanette
made a necklace by stringing the shiny brown chinquapins
on fishing line with a big needle.

Corn turned brown in the fields. Clumps of staghorn
sumac stood on the roadbanks, like herds of deer looking
down. Leaves rattled on the trees. Grandpa Smith went to
the Bearwallow for a week with his fox-hunting buddies.
When I got up early to feed Bertie and milk the cows the
first morning he was gone, frost covered the ground.

I was sitting by the woodstove that evening reading my
poetry book when Clyde Cox and his brother Columbus
and a bunch more came by the house and called me out to

go coon hunting with them. They waited at the edge of the yard, with their lanterns and flashlights, their dogs whining and straining on leashes. It was still a week until Halloween, but Jeanette had already made two jack-o'-lanterns and put candles in them, and they were grinning at the edge of the yard, too. While I went back inside and asked Mom if I could go hunting, Eugene and Jeanette looked out at all the lights, their noses pressed to windowpanes.

"Who is it?" Mom wanted to know.

I said it was Clyde Cox and his brother Columbus, and some others that hung around Grandpa Wells's store. Weaver and Everett Sams, Ernest Barnes, Kermit Worley.

"Lord, what a crowd!" Mom said.

I said I pitched horseshoes with them all the time.

"I thought all the hunters were in the Bearwallow, with your grandpa," Grandma Smith said.

"This is coon huntin', not fox huntin'," I explained.

"You've got no business going off huntin', especially with your grandpa not here," Mom said. "Besides, it's a school night."

"What would we do if somebody broke in on us?" Grandma Smith said.

"Nobody's going to break in, and we won't be gone long, we're just goin' up on Horse Knob and around close," I said, grabbing my coat and giving all the excuses and explanations I could as fast as I could. I knew the hunters out in the yard wouldn't wait long for me.

"Don't leave without your hat," Mom said, and I knew I had her permission, even if it was grudging. "It's cold out there. And don't you be gone long."

I put my hat on and turned the fur flaps down over my ears, just to reassure Mom. Five minutes later I was climbing the ridge above our house, my breath coming in clouds, a hunter among hunters. Overhead stars gave off a hard gleam, as if the sky had been driven full of new nails.

Still hardly believing they had asked me to go with them, I kept quiet and listened. "I never can go coon huntin' without thinking of old Gerald Scott, off up there in Michigan," Columbus Cox said. "Last time ever I did see him, we went coon huntin' up in here together."

"He left for Michigan the next morning," Everett Sams said. "Never has been back, I reckon."

"I recollect how old Gerald used to sing. 'Ring-dang-doo, what is that? Round and fuzzy like a pussy cat.' "

"What's that he would sing?" I said.

Columbus Cox laughed. "Little Wells here don't know the ring-dang-doo."

"He will," Everett Sams said.

But nobody explained what they were talking about. They just went on talking about something else.

"There's a whole bunch of us from around here up north now—Dayton, Ohio. Flint, Michigan."

"We've branched out along the blacktop roads like a vine growing out a forked limb," Jess Barnes said. "I got two brothers up there. They draw back in here when times is hard up there. Or let something strike here, and they shake too."

"I reckon we're the root and they're the stem," Kermit Worley said. "All them from around here that's gone off up there to work. I tried it, but I soon give out gettin' used to it."

"Old Gerald must've liked it. He never has been back."

We crossed a high pasture, stopped at the edge of the woods, and unleashed the dogs—Jess Barnes's black-and-tan and Clyde Cox's two coonhounds. "Whooee!" Clyde hollered, as the eager hounds bounded noisily off through the leaves.

"They're right tonight!" Kermit Worley said. He winked at me. "Little Wells, that dog of Jess's may just tree us a bear."

"He's got beardog in him," Clyde said. "But he's trained for coon."

I'd gone fox hunting with Grandpa Smith, and what we did was sit in one place and listen to the hounds chase the fox. Grandpa Smith didn't want the hounds ever to catch the fox, he just liked to hear them run. Coon hunting was different, though; we wanted to catch the coon. But after we turned the hounds loose, we sat a long time waiting for them to strike a trail, just as we did when I went fox hunting with Grandpa Smith.

While we waited, the talk flowed on, like a creek running. "I dearly love to hunt," Kermit Worley said. "But I do believe I like to fish better. I tell you what I like to do. I like to get me something to drink, drop it in a cooler, get me some bait, but not these two-cent crickets, or these nightcrawlers like they sell around Big Ivy Lake over there—that's baitin' your hook with a dime every time. Bagworms, they're good when you can find some, and I usually can. Or a big wasper's nest. And I like to drive down past Lucas in my pickup, catch me a mess of bluegills, some little channel cats. You like to fish, Little Wells?"

I said I'd fished in the creek, and Dad had taken Eugene, Jeanette, and me fishing at his trout pond on Spring Creek, but I never had been fishing in Big Ivy Lake.

"You'll have to go with me sometime. Lord, I've fished off the rocks there at that place they call The Narrows,

when it was coming dark, moon already on the water. . . .
I recollect once there was this cloud, big cloud, just as blue
and soft as mole fur, and the reflection of it there on the
water looked to me like a sea horse or something you're apt
to come on in a book, like that book you're always readin'
in, Little Wells. That one I seen you readin' in at your
granddaddy's store."

Kermit kidded me about reading poetry. Sometimes I'd
read him something from the book Grandma Wells gave
me, the way I read to Grandpa Smith, and Kermit would
roll his eyes. But he seemed to think it was all right for me
to read poetry, because I was a Wells, and my father worked
for a congressman. He figured if I kept on reading poetry
books I'd probably make a congressman, too.

"Listen," Clyde Cox said.

We listened a long time; finally, Clyde said he must have
just thought he heard one of his hounds.

"Yeah, I like to come home with a mess of fish and have
a midnight supper," Kermit said.

I wondered what it would be like to be grown-up, like
Kermit Worley. He lived alone and drove Grandpa Wells's
rolling store, a big aluminum box built on the frame of a
ton-and-a-half Ford truck, that ran regular routes up half
the creeks in Madison and Bunker counties. I thought it
would be great to come in late at night with a string of fish
and fry them up at midnight.

Then Clyde did hear one of his hounds strike a trail. We
all heard it. His other hound joined in.

"They're trailin'!"

"Listen," Clyde said. "When you hear 'em start to bay,
right regular, you'll know they have it up a tree. That's
how they sound when they're barkin' treed."

The dogs hadn't trailed more than three or four minutes before they began to bay, barking treed, just as Clyde said they would.

"That's no coon, I'll bet you money," Jess Barnes said. "Never trailed long enough for it to be a coon. And my Trigg dog never trailed with 'em. He won't bother with a possum."

We moved down through the woods to where the dogs sat baying under a dogwood. Somebody shined a light up in the tree. Sure enough, it was a possum. Its eyes gleamed in the light.

"Now watch this," Columbus Cox said. He swung himself up into the dogwood, reached out and got hold of the limb the possum was in, and shook the possum loose. It hit the ground and started to run away, but one of the black-and-tan hounds grabbed it at the neck. The possum rolled up into a ball of gray fur. Clyde took the possum by the tail and dropped it into a sack he pulled from his coat pocket.

Clyde's brother Columbus scooted down out of the dogwood and brushed himself off. "Don't that beat all you ever seen?" he said. "These dogs will sull a possum, like that, and never break the skin. That's how they're trained. When a dog's not trained right, it'll just tear into a possum and ruin the hide, but not these here dogs."

We went on through the woods, urging the hounds ahead of us. Weaver Sams got to telling about somebody he'd worked for, somebody named Gillum, who was stripping for coal over in east Bunker.

"I thought old Gillum was against strip-minin'," Jess Barnes said.

"He was—till he found out his land had a big coal seam on it. Now he's stripped in there above his house, and when it rains, mud and rocks and trees wash down. It's just about washed his house away."

"Said he prayed over it, and the Lord told him to strip it!"

"I don't believe the Lord said any such thing!"

"That was old Gillum whisperin' to hisself!"

"They always said Gillum was like the moon—got a dark side to him, never lets his light side know what his dark side's doin'."

"He's rich now, though."

"I heard he's bought a airplane."

"Rich, yeah. But he's rurnt that land of his."

"They say it's not safe to hunt where there's been strip-minin'. You're apt to walk right over a highwall—just like steppin' off a cliff."

"You better believe it. If you hunt where the land's been stripped, you'd better know where you are, where the high-walls are."

"Listen!"

"Here we go!" Jess Barnes said. "That there's my Trigg; he's struck something."

Soon Clyde Cox's black-and-tans joined Jess's dog, and they trailed as we followed, stopping now and then to listen.

"If that was a possum, they'd have it treed by now," Jess said. "Besides, Trigg never would have given mouth on the trail of a possum."

"They're trailin' up from that bluff by the branch."

We commenced to climb the ridge. By the time we reached the tree where the dogs sat baying, looking up, we were all breathing hard, blowing great clouds of breath.

"Lord, what a tree!"

"Big white oak."

"Let's see what's up there."

"Shine a light. Kermit, throw the beam of that big six-cell of yours up in there."

"That light'll reach to the moon!"

Kermit raked the trunk of the white oak with the beam of his light, moved it along first one limb, then another.

"Keep lookin'."

"A coon knows to hide his eyes—so the light won't pick him up. Possums, now, they don't know to do that. I shined a light up in a tree once, and it was this old mama possum with her little possums, seven or eight of them, hangin' on to her. So many of 'em, when my light hit all their eyes, that tree lit up like a Christmas tree!"

"Well, where is he?"

"He's up there," Jess Barnes said. "He's there somewhere. My Trigg won't lie. He won't say he's got a coon up a tree just because he thinks you want him to. If he barks treed, there's a coon up there, I guarantee."

"There! Right there. No, back down a little. There, see!"

Finally, I saw the coon, its brownish gray body and the black rings on its tail.

"Boys, he couldn't a-gone much higher!"

"Who's gonna shake this one? Columbus?"

"Not me. A feller'll have to scoot out on that limb to shake that coon out. Limb's not big enough to hold me. Need somebody light."

"Little Wells, how about it?"

"You're the lightest one."

I knew I had to climb the tree. If I didn't, they might not ask me to go hunting with them again. And though it looked to me to be five hundred feet to the limb the coon sat on, I had to climb there—somehow. Jess Barnes and Kermit Worley made a cradle with their hands and hoisted me as high as they could, and I started climbing. I was a long time, while they all shouted encouragement from below. Their voices grew fainter and fainter. Finally, I reached the limb the coon sat on. I held tight, resting.

From where I sat, astraddle the limb as if it were a saddle, I could see the dark ridges running east. I thought how, just a couple of hours ago, I'd been sitting by the warm woodstove at Grandma and Grandpa Smith's, reading my poetry book, and now, suddenly, I found myself high up in a white oak, on a frosty night in October. I sat higher than when we rode the Ferris wheel at the carnival and it stopped with us right on top. I sat so high I could see back across the ridges to Grandma and Grandpa Smith's. I could see over into east Bunker, where the man they called Gillum had strip-mined the land. I'd been afraid at first, and now I felt a little homesick, for I figured I was looking over into Bunker County, maybe all the way to Dayton and Flint and Detroit, where Gerald Scott and all the others from Madison had gone to work. But more than anything, I was glad I'd climbed the white oak. Sitting on that high limb felt a little like sitting in the saddle astride a huge horse. Gasping the cold night air, my face flushed from the long climb and from amazement, I began to shake the limb.

⇛ 22 ⇚

"THAT NEVER HAPPENED," I said.

"Shore, it did," Jess Barnes said, and cut his eyes at Kermit Worley.

We were over at the foot of Hanlon Mountain, up the holler past an old tenant house that belonged to Grandpa Wells, coon hunting again, waiting for the black-and-tans to strike a trail. It was Halloween. Jess Barnes had been telling about Wiley Woods and Junior Crumm going to Columbus, Ohio, to look for work, and getting their car compacted into a little bale of metal by mistake at a junk-yard. "That's just a tale you're tellin'," I said.

"And I guess it never happened about old man Bob Elton's boy," Jess said.

"What?" I asked.

And Jess was off and running with another tale. "Why, down yonder at the forks of the creek, by the mailboxes and the swinging bridge, back years ago, a mad dog bit old man Elton's boy—laid the boy's eyeball down on his face, bloodied him up. Course, all that was years before. But I was on my way from an all-night coon hunt, like this one, only it was just at daybreak on a foggy morning in August. There was a burley tobacco patch ripening in that branch bank bottom, and I was coming home, thinking about how every foggy morning in August was supposed to foretell a snow that winter—coming along there, and I saw two kids, both of them barefooted, both in overalls, looking enough alike to be twin brothers, saw them cross on that swinging bridge, looking back over their shoulder, like maybe something was following them. They went along the Elton Branch road there—I stood watching them—and then, just like that, they were gone. They didn't turn off the road or anything, they just melted into nothing and they were gone.

"Now, I'd heard tell that people had seen the Elton boy's ghost along there where the mad dog had bit him. Only it couldn't a been his ghost, because he wasn't dead, people just thought he was. He was down around Franklin in this state hospital. He didn't go mad from the dog bite—they give him shots against that—but he went sort of crazy. Never was right in his mind after he got bit. But people thought he was dead, don't you see. I never had believed in ghosts or any such, but now I'd seen what I'd seen. And I couldn't figure it—how come they's two boys instead of one? And I got to thinking, and remembering the times when I'd been so scared, I thought me up a brother, or a buddy, to talk to in the dark, or to go with me through some snaky place.

"Back then, though, I never told anybody about seeing them two boys, crossing that swinging bridge at daybreak, not even after I saw them a second time, once in March or early April, and again down in November—about this time of year."

"Is that the truth?" I asked.

"Yes, sir, but I never told it till I was a grown man. Nobody would have believed me when I was a tadwhacker like you. You have to pass that way on your way back home this morning, don't you, Little Wells?"

"I don't have to," I said.

"You know, they say sometimes they still let that one-eyed Elton boy come home from the state hospital."

"I could go another way," I said.

Headed home just at daybreak, my shoes crunching frosted grass, I did pass by the mailboxes and the swinging bridge, and I thought about the ghost-boys, though I didn't see them. But feverish from having stayed up all night, my thoughts racing, I was ready to see anything. I came into the yard at Grandma and Grandpa Smith's, where Jeanette's two snaggle-toothed jack-o'-lanterns grinned at me, their candles burned short. I took off my shoes on the porch and stepped quietly into the house without waking anyone. I slept, and dreamed blood and fire. In my dream, Columbus, Ohio, and Detroit, Michigan, were just over the hill, where cars collided and burst into flames that lit up the night sky.

➳➳➳ 23 ⬳⬳⬳

A FTER I STARTED HUNTING at night, my world widened. I started hanging out at Grandpa Wells's store, where Clyde Cox and Jess Barnes and the men and boys I hunted with came and went. Clyde and his brother had a truck; they made a living cutting timber and pulpwood. I worked for them in the afternoons. I rode with them in their jeeps and trucks up other creeks I'd only heard about, and went other places I'd never even heard of. I still lived with my mom, and Eugene and Jeanette, and Grandma and Grandpa Smith, and my grandma and grandpa Wells lived further down the road—but that world receded and began to seem small compared to the larger world I was exploring.

I got a job stocking Grandpa Wells's rolling store afternoons and evenings after school. A big aluminum box built on the frame of a ton-and-a-half Ford truck, the rolling store was Grandpa Wells's idea. He said if people couldn't get to the Trading Post, he'd get the Trading Post to them. Kermit Worley drove the rolling store on regular routes up half the creeks in Madison and Bunker counties. On Saturdays I'd ride with Kermit on his route. People met us at the big road bringing butter and eggs they traded for coffee, sugar, salt, and plug tobacco. They traded hides and sassafras bark for snuff and baking powders; bloodroot and yellow dock or a little ginseng for needles, can lids, BC headache powders, and toothache medicine.

I seldom went home except to sleep. I'd get off the school bus at Grandpa Wells's store, and when I finished stocking with Kermit for the next day's run, I'd go hunting with whoever was going, or, if no one was going, I'd hang around the store until it closed. Mom didn't seem to mind, although she said I spent so much time at the store I might just as well get me a cot and sleep there, too.

"Maybe I will," I said, kidding her. "And when you learn to drive, you can come see me!" She had told me that Carlene Cantrell was teaching her how to drive—or at least trying to.

Something was always happening at the store. And you never knew who was going to pull in.

THE SUTHERLANDS PULLED up at Grandpa Wells's on a cold January afternoon right after New Year's. I had finished stocking the rolling store and was sitting close to the stove with some of the others—all of us in blue-denim jeans and jackets and plaid shirts, and hats with furry earflaps. Everybody sat humped up on Pepsi crates and nail kegs—hunted out, talked out, winter-bound. We'd all heard each other's lies a hundred times, all the moldy jokes and comebacks. All we felt like doing was sitting and listening to the Dixie

Dew syrup bucket, half-full of water, singing on the coal stove. The coal bucket, with two lumps of coal and half an orange peel, had more on its mind than we had on ours.

Then the Sutherlands pulled up. Grady Plemmons said, "I wished you'd look a-yonder!"

We looked up, like hounds stirred out of sleep.

The Sutherlands just appeared—in an old gray panel truck that had once been some kind of company truck; lettering on the sides had been painted over. The truck smoked out the busted muffler, it shuddered going into gear, and the fenders flapped up and down, like a buzzard trying to fly up off the road. Idling, the motor sounded like two dozen empty coathangers swinging and swaying and crashing together in a closet.

The old gray panel truck was packed full of Sutherlands. ("Like coons in a holler log," Grady Plemmons said later.) They came into the store, and came, and came, and just kept coming, twelve or thirteen of them, finally, and that still left an old woman on the front seat of the panel truck, her head bobbing up and down like a bird pecking about in gravel.

They crowded in: old man Sutherland in overalls, a brown suitcoat and black felt hat; Miz Sutherland—we figured—a red bandanna for a kerchief, her thin face like an ax blade with a piece broken out; a pregnant girl who could have been fifteen or thirty, wearing a pair of men's pants and a checkered shirt that barely reached over her protruding stomach. Behind her came a girl who could have been her twin, except she wasn't expecting; a man, thirty, maybe, crippled, who smiled and looked right past us, like a blind man. Then came the kids, milling, sniffing, pressing against one another, running back to the truck, getting change from the old woman with the bobbing head. A man old enough to be her father stayed right by the pregnant girl. He wore slacks and a suitcoat and sharp-toed city shoes, had long gray sideburns, black hair combed straight back, and gray chest hairs at his open collar.

We couldn't tell who was with whom, or how they all shook out, exactly. Later Grady Plemmons said they probably didn't know, either. But you knew they were a family; they all went together somehow—pieces of a puzzle that made one picture.

Grady Plemmons was the better part of an hour waiting on them. They bought things separately, even the children. The old man bought two dollars worth of gas and four quarts of bulk oil for the panel truck. He started it by having the two younger men push, then he caught the motor with the clutch. As soon as they were gone, we started talking. All of us, all at once. Grady Plemmons, Everett and Weaver Sams, Clyde and Columbus Cox, Jess Barnes, Kermit Worley. Grady put more coal in the stove and didn't even notice that we laughed and talked long past closing time.

"I feel a whole lot better just having something to talk about," Jess Barnes said.

"You mean some*body* to talk about!" Clyde Cox said.

Kermit Worley laughed. "It's the truth! I tell you, before that crowd come in, I felt like forty miles of bad road. I was lower than a snake's belly in a side ditch. That crowd pert-near saved my life!"

We got to know Earl Sutherland, the crippled man. Earl would smile and look right past you and tell you everything you wanted to know. And we wanted to know everything.

What we found out was that earlier that day, before they first came in the store, they had already been by Grandpa Wells's and arranged with him to move into a house he owned further on up the creek, at the foot of Hanlon Mountain, an old house nobody had lived in for years. It had been Grandpa Wells who steered them toward his own store to do their trading.

Crippled Earl told us that when he came in the store a day or two later with a suitcase full of rabbits, neatly gutted, with the fur still on—flat rabbits frozen stiff as sticks of stovewood. He'd caught them all in deadfalls, Earl said, grinning. He figured to carry them on the bus to Mountain City, peddle them door to door, for fifty cents apiece.

Earl told us about his brother, Clayton, who'd been killed by a cousin years ago. They'd been digging a groundhog out of a den when Clayton saw the hog and jumped at it just as his cousin brought the mattock down—and split Clayton's head wide open. And there was Darla, a sister who accidentally drank turpentine and died when she was two.

Earl even showed us his crippled foot. There was a flap cut in the side of his brogan. A white cloth showed through. Under the cloth was a hole in Earl's left foot, just below the anklebone, a hurt that would not heal.

Crippled Earl kept us posted about all the Sutherlands. They didn't aim to make a crop. They hunted, trapped, dug ginseng, cut pulpwood and fenceposts, worked in timber. All up and down Newfound Creek we'd see the Sutherlands going into the woods or coming out, the whole tribe, even old Grandma. They moved up the branch banks on cold days gathering cresses. We'd see them out in a field, like a flock of starlings, or just standing at the edge of the woods somewhere, like cattle with their backs turned to the wind.

Later on, when the sap was rising, the Sutherlands swarmed the branch banks cutting willows. We'd see them going along, their backs bent under bundles of willows. "Makin' baskets," Crippled Earl said, grinning. "Baskets and chairs."

They made good chairs and baskets, too—and peddled them, cheap, from the panel truck. There wasn't anyone on Newfound who didn't buy a chair of woven willow, or at least a dollar basket. They peddled chairs and baskets on all the creeks around there—on Sandy Mush, Hogeye. Then as suddenly as they'd come, the Sutherlands left, like a swarm of bees, leaving Grandpa Wells's old house at the foot of Hanlon Mountain like an empty bee gum—moved on over toward Dillsboro somewhere, we heard, not long after the girl who was fifteen going on thirty had her baby. I thought of Mom, and how young she'd been when I was born.

But even after they left, the Sutherlands kept on making us feel better when we loafed around Grandpa Wells's Trading Post in the evening. There wasn't a one of us who could make more of a willow limb than a whistle, or a pile of stupid shavings at our feet. But, sitting in the willow chairs the Sutherlands had made—Grady bought half a dozen of them for the store—we knew we sat higher, somehow, than they did.

I remembered what Grandma Wells had said about the two kinds of people, the good livers and the sorry, and I figured we were acting like the good people and making the

Sutherlands out to be sorry. But I still couldn't accept it, for I didn't see how the Sutherlands could be sorry. They worked, they were friendly, and they could make good chairs and baskets. They were a family. Yet we sat around and made fun of them. I felt ashamed, going along with it.

≫ 24 ≪

EVERY SATURDAY THAT SPRING and for a year after, I rode with Kermit Worley, sitting high in his cab, going up the gravel roads that ran beside the creeks and sometimes through them, roads so little traveled that weeds grew up between the ruts, like the balk between untended corn rows.

I'd see the Sutherland's willow chairs on porches, out under trees in yards. I thought of the time Dad made all those cement blocks and peddled them to everyone on New-found Creek. I could still see those blocks, too, when I went up and down the roads.

Kermit always tried to fix me up with girls who came out of the hollers to meet our rolling store. I halfway liked the ribbing and Kermit knew it. "These hollers is full of gals—good-lookin' gals, too," he'd say. His cigarette bobbed up and down, and ashes fell onto the seat between his legs. "Yes, sir! Good-lookin' gals, by golly!" he'd shout over the groan of the motor pulling in first gear.

I changed the subject. "Where is it they're strip-mining?"

I asked. We were over in the edge of Bunker County. Mrs. Slone, my history teacher at West Madison Consolidated, had been talking in class about strip-mining in Bunker County and how it was destroying the mountains.

"That's further on over, further than we go," Kermit said.

One morning in June on Beaverdam, we came pulling hard around a turn and Kermit said, "Looky yonder!" By a bridge over a branch where a brand-new, tin-roofed barn gleamed in a little flat, a girl in blue jeans and a yellow blouse stood in an apple tree, out on a thick lower limb. She looked at us and held to another limb overhead. "I tell you," Kermit said, "gals grow on trees up here!"

By the time we stopped, the girl was standing on the ground. Kermit swung open the big back doors, climbed up, and took her butter and strawberries, and while she traded, he played matchmaker. He told the girl I'd come all the way up there looking for a healthy gal. The girl and I exchanged embarrassed glances. I told her I went to West Madison School, and she told me she attended East Bunker. That was all we ever said to one another. But back down at Grandpa Wells's store, Kermit told how he had taken me where girls grew on trees, where all a feller had to do was shake them off, like apples.

I hunted and fished, and kept the rolling store stocked. Still I had time, that fall when I started tenth grade and turned fifteen, to work in timber and pulpwood for the men and boys I hunted with. Eugene was milking the cows at home now and helping Grandpa Smith with the tobacco. Jeanette was becoming a little Grandma Smith; she could cook and sew and do everything Grandma Smith could do—even make quilts and baskets. She won a prize at school with a quilt she made.

Mom had started going for rides with Walter Lee Rogers, her boss at Blue Ridge Manufacturing. All Mom talked about that spring I was finishing tenth grade was Walter Lee. She was always imitating the slow way Walter Lee talked and predicting what Walter Lee would say about something. I asked Mom if she and Walter Lee were going to get married. She began to twist her foot and talk pleasurably about how slow Walter Lee was. She said Walter Lee told her he'd been thinking about asking her to go for a ride for six months before he actually asked her. Grandma Smith said Walter Lee might be slow, but she believed he was a good man. She knew the Rogerses. The Rogers men tended to marry late, in their late thirties and early forties; it was just their way.

→≫ ≪←

ONE AFTERNOON THAT SUMMER I was fifteen, Dad stopped by Grandpa Wells's store on his way to Bunker County. I wanted to ride over there with him, but he wasn't sure I should go. He was going to pay his respects, and Congressman Hatcher's, to the family of Artis Oldham, who had died. Dad had gone to school with Artis Oldham.

"You don't need to go over there," Dad said. "It's a sad occasion."

But I said I understood that, and he let me go.

We had ridden only a little while when Dad said, "Artis didn't just die. He shot himself."

"Why?"

"It's hard to know what's in a man's mind and heart."

We were both quiet a long time as we drove along the gravel road that turned beside the creek. I began to notice bullet-riddled road signs that seemed to say, "This is the way to the house of the suicide."

"Are we going to be going where they strip-mine?" I asked Dad.

He said we would be passing some strip-mining, but the worst of it was back off the county roads. You had to get on the haul roads and drive back over the ridges to see most of it.

But soon, for the first time, I saw what Mrs. Slone had already described in class: the top of a mountain shaved off on both sides, with a strip of trees left in the middle, like a Mohawk haircut; gashes cut around the sides of hills, with trees uprooted and pushed down into the hollers along with huge boulders. Where the road topped a ridge I could see down a long valley that looked like it had been bombed. When we descended and drove along close by the creek, I could see that the water was black with acid runoff.

"How can they just come in and tear everything up like this?" I asked.

"They can if they own the mineral rights," Dad said.

Then I remembered Mrs. Slone had said that mineral rights had been sold a long time ago, before anyone ever dreamed there could be such a thing as strip-mining, with bulldozers and great shovels. But the contracts said the owner of the mineral rights could extract the coal any way he wanted to.

"Still, it's not right," I said.

We left the road, pulled through a set of cattle bars, topped a dusty ridge. Far below I could see several cars bunched tightly between a house and a tin-topped shed, gleaming in the sun like a school of minnows in a pool of light. Soon Dad and I were standing with men gathered in the shade of trees, talking quietly, whittling, spitting into the dust. Dad went around shaking hands with everybody. I wandered about, listening to what the several small groups of men were saying. They seemed to agree that liquor had been Artis Oldham's problem. "He didn't drink liquor, liquor drunk him."

I studied my reflection distorted in a shiny hubcap: a long face set on tiny legs, a brown-eyed dwarf escaped from a crazy, hung over brain just before a bullet spattered red mud over the picture. Artis Oldham had come out on the porch, stood with his hand in his pocket, stepped down beside the rosebushes—those rosebushes right over there —and shot himself. I thought of him falling like the mud-splattered hubcap, rolling in tighter and tighter circles, slowing, wobbling, lying finally face down. Where he bled, someone had thrown a shovelful of sand.

I wandered out to where fenceposts staggered down the hill. Where the posts with their tangled, rusty barbed wire finally lay on the ground above a row of empty bee gums, I stopped. The bees must have known something and left, or else they'd starved out in winter. Grandma Smith said bees knew if something bad was about to happen, and if somebody died, you were supposed to tell the bees about it. But there were no bees left here to tell anything to.

Behind the shed, cans and bottles tumbled into a ditch. Beyond the shed sat an old black Chevrolet truck up to its axle in silt, its windshield and every window shot through. The splintered glass around each hole had the symmetry of spiderwebs. Rust bled from bullet holes in the fenders and the left front door. The old truck must have been used for target practice.

Wandering on to the barn, I found whiskey bottles stuck between logs. In a barrel in the corner of a dark stall, tobacco sticks and more bottles. A rat's nest in a wide-mouthed mason jar.

I stood again in the circle of spit and whittle, smelling new overalls. Then we all went into the house—I stayed close to Dad—where Artis Oldham lay in a coffin between two sprays of flowers. His hands were crossed on his stomach. Four fingers on his right hand looked like those clay tubes mud daubers build in toolsheds, cribs, barns—tubes stuffed full of stunned spiders, and the eggs that hatch to eat them. The funeral flowers had a whiskey breath.

On the way back to Grandpa Wells's store, I told Dad what I'd heard the men saying—that liquor made Artis Oldham kill himself.

"Liquor didn't help matters," Dad said. "But that's not the whole story. The Black Gold Coal Company's getting ready to strip-mine Artis's place."

"Couldn't you or Congressman Hatcher stop them?"

Dad cocked his head to one side and smiled a crooked smile. "Hatcher represents both sides—the people against strip-mining, and the people for it. Besides, it's what the law says now that counts, and Artis had gone to court—and lost."

"Then there ought to be a different law," I said.

Dad said it would be difficult to get the law changed, or to get a new one. "But I believe that's why Artis shot himself. I believe he couldn't bear to see the place strip-mined . . . torn up . . . ruined. Hard to say, though."

I remembered what Dad had said: it was hard to know what was in a person's mind and heart. I thought about the empty bee gums at Artis Oldham's, with their tops scattered around the side of the hill. I remembered the time, soon after Mom moved us back there, when Grandma Smith had prevented a swarm of Grandpa's bees from escaping to the mountain by running after them, beating a pie pan with a spoon, making a clatter that caused the bees to settle on a pine bough and stay there until Grandpa Smith came and put them in a new bee gum.

The way Grandma had talked, bees were like people. They made their home, worked together like a family, and stored honey, the way we stored apples and pears and potatoes for the winter. And bees seemed to know things, like people. They knew when it was time to move, and leave the hive behind and find a new place. Maybe there hadn't been anybody at Artis Oldham's, like Grandma Smith, to keep the bees from leaving.

I used to sit and try to figure out why Mom and Dad got divorced, and whose fault it was. I'd blame first Mom, then Dad, then Mom again. Now I didn't blame either one of them. Instead, I wondered if Mom and Dad hadn't known it was time to move, and leave our house standing like an empty beehive. I thought of Mom and Eugene and Jeanette and me moving to Grandma and Grandpa Smith's, like bees swarming.

And I wondered what had been in Artis Oldham's mind and heart . . . if the bulldozers would ever come to Newfound Creek to cut up the mountains, topple the trees, and make the waters of Newfound Creek run black.

⇶ 25 ⇷

I WAS TAKING a shortcut back from Grandpa Wells's store late one Saturday afternoon after I'd been up South Turkey Creek with Kermit Worley on the rolling store. It was well into July, and coming along the old wagon road that ran below the apple orchard back of Grandpa Smith's barn, I noticed that apples on the trees were weighing the branches down. Grandpa Smith, I saw, had propped up some of the branches with forked poles to keep the limbs from breaking with the weight of apples. I stopped suddenly, for I saw something else. A car had left the wagon road and nosed into a ditch. The back wheels were spinning, and blue smoke rose off them. Who could have driven down here? As I ran toward the car, I saw it was Carlene Cantrell's.

I stopped about ten yards from the blue two-door Chevrolet and stood listening to the engine race and the rear wheels whine as they spun and smoked and threw red clay out of the ditch. I stepped closer and saw Mom sitting on the passenger side! Carlene sat behind the wheel. Mom was looking over at Carlene, so neither of them saw me until I walked up and pecked on Mom's window. She jumped and looked startled. I motioned for her to roll down the window.

"We're in a pickle, I tell you!" Carlene said, letting the car idle.

"How'd you get down in there?" I asked.

"It was easy!" Carlene said.

"Now, Carlene," Mom said, "I'm not letting you take the blame for this. I ran us off in here," she said to me. She looked the way Jeanette used to look when she spilled milk at the table. "Carlene wouldn't have done this. She's a good driver."

"I was teachin' your mother to drive," Carlene said. "We come off down here where there wouldn't be anything to run into—we thought!"

"I don't know what happened," Mom said. "I was doing all right, and then the front wheels just came up out of a rut back there, and the steering wheel started going every which way, and the next thing I knew—"

"I believe you mashed the gas more, instead of the brake," Carlene said. "Seemed like we just kept gettin' faster!"

"Oh, I wish I never had started this!" Mom said.

"Now, Nora, you hush that! This ain't nothin'. Could have happened to anybody. You should have seen me when I was tryin' to learn!"

"I think I broke something," Mom said. "We've been trying to get out for fifteen minutes."

"You didn't break anything!" Carlene said. "We're just down in a ditch." Carlene seemed to be having great fun. "Maybe if you stood on the back bumper, Robert."

I stood on the back bumper. Carlene raced the motor. The tires whined and smoked and sent red clay flying. It wasn't working, so I hollered for Carlene to stop.

"Maybe if Mom and I both stood on the bumper," I said.

Mom got out of the car and stood on the back bumper with me. Carlene raced the motor and again the tires whined and smoked and flung red clay. That didn't work, either.

"I saw Columbus Cox rock his pickup out of a place where he got stuck," I said.

"Rock it?" Carlene said.

"You get out and let me see if I can do it," I said.

"Robert, you don't know how to drive," Mom said.

I said I did know how to drive. Kermit Worley taught me some, and also Grandpa Wells. I had been driving Grandpa Wells's truck—but not on the highway. Well, twice I'd driven it on the highway, down to Grandpa Wells's store, but he had been in the truck with me.

"You don't have a license!" Mom said.

"But I'm going to get one in three months, when I'm sixteen."

Carlene and Mom stood back while I spun the wheels in reverse, quickly shifted to low gear, then back to reverse again. I did that over and over until I had the car rocking backward and forward. Once the rear wheels made it almost to the top of the ditch, but then the rear end slipped sideways.

"Stop!" Mom said. "If you get it any more sideways, it's apt to turn over!"

I left the car idling, got out, and stood with them trying to think what could be done. I'd seen people put planks under the wheels of stuck cars and come right out on the planks. But we didn't have any planks.

"Do you think Bertie could pull it out?" Mom said.

I figured she could. I could go harness Bertie up and hook a log chain to the back bumper.

"But I wouldn't want Papa to know!" Mom said. "Can you get Bertie around here without Papa seeing?"

I said I'd try. I walked on around the old road and came out between the barn and the house. Bertie stood in the pasture, but there was Grandpa Smith, too, chopping wood in the woodlot. I couldn't catch Bertie, lead her to the barn, and harness her without Grandpa Smith seeing me. But if Mom and Carlene didn't get out of the ditch soon, it would be getting dark.

I walked below the woodlot where Grandpa Smith was chopping, keeping his back to me, got my bicycle, and went flying down the long drive. Looking both ways as I came to the big road, I turned right onto it and started pedaling hard on the blacktop. Less than five minutes later I scooted to a stop by Grandpa Wells's toolshed, frightening Tom, Grandpa Wells's big peacock, who shrieked and spread his tail feathers the way I'd seen Dad fan out a whole deck of cards with one hand. Grandpa Wells's car was gone. I'd hoped it would be. He and Grandma Wells had probably gone to town.

I knew where the spare key to his old farm truck hung, on a post under the shed. I got it, started the truck, and backed it out. I was headed down the drive when I remembered I didn't have a chain. So I backed up, got a big heavy one out of the shed, and started down the drive again.

Now, how was I going to manage this? I couldn't drive the truck past Grandpa Smith's. He'd see the truck easier than he would have seen me harnessing Bertie. There was a gate, I remembered, at the other end of the old wagon road. I could open that gate, and bring the truck in to where Mom and Carlene were stuck without having to go past Grandpa Smith's.

Mom and Carlene were expecting to see me coming down the wagon road, with Bertie. Instead, I came up the road in Grandpa Wells's truck.

"What in the world?" Mom said. "Where's Bertie?"

I explained that I couldn't get Bertie without Grandpa seeing me.

"You drove on the road—and you with no license!" Mom said, looking at Grandpa Wells's truck.

"I had to—or else come by Grandpa Smith's. The ox was in the ditch, as Grandma Smith would say."

"I wish you'd listen!" Carlene said. "He's callin' us oxen!"

Mom wasn't in a mood to joke. "I'm going to get us *all* in trouble!" she said.

I hooked one end of the chain to the frame of the truck, back under the bed, and the other end to the rear bumper of Carlene's Chevrolet.

"Now, you go easy!" Mom said, standing back, a hand held to the side of her face.

Carlene got in her car, started it up. Her round face at the open side window beamed back at me. "Give it the gas!" she called.

Looking back, I eased forward in low gear until the chain tightened and Carlene's Chevrolet rocked a little. Wondering if even the truck would pull the car out, I accelerated. The old motor coughed, began to roar throatily, the gears groaned, and Carlene's Chevrolet came right up out of the ditch into the old wagon road and stopped.

Mom stood at a distance clapping.

"We sure skinned that cat!" Carlene said, getting out of her car. "You did real good, Robert!"

While I unhooked the chain, Mom apologized to Carlene for getting her into such a fix. That did it, Mom said. She was finished with trying to learn to drive. She was quitting—before she tore up Carlene's car, or got both of them hurt, or worse.

"I want you to listen!" Carlene said. "Why, honey, this ain't nothin'. When I was learnin', I done everything but climb trees with my brother's old car! You're not quittin'! I'll not let you! Why, you learned how to typewrite, just like playin' a piano. And you'll get the hang of drivin', too!"

Carlene and Mom followed me out the back way, through the cattle gate. Grandpa and Grandma Wells still weren't back from town when I returned the truck. I parked it under the big shed, hung the key on the post, and rode my bicycle back up to Grandma and Grandpa Smith's.

Mom was home already. At supper she gave me knowing looks.

⇛26⇚

I'D LEARNED FROM CRIPPLED Earl Sutherland how to make a deadfall. He showed me how he trapped muskrat and mink in Newfound Creek, and I'd bought half a dozen steel traps from him before the Sutherlands moved on. I knew Grandpa Smith wouldn't like it if I set them for foxes, because he wanted the foxes around for his hounds to chase. Also, he didn't want me setting traps in the woods because his foxhounds might wander into them and ruin their feet. He'd even gone along the creek with me and showed me good places to set them. But after I had seen the pelts of the two red foxes Crippled Earl had caught, I wanted to trap foxes, too. I knew I shouldn't, but I set the traps anyway, come fall, in dens and on trails in the bluff above Grandpa Smith's. I could run my trapline quickly after I got home from school, and before I went to work at the Trading Post. If I needed to, I could also get up early and run the trapline before the school bus came.

I still didn't like West Madison Consolidated as much as I'd liked our old Newfound School. Bells rang and locker doors banged every fifty minutes, and the principal and the coaches interrupted classes with the public-address system so often it was hard for the teachers to teach. The town kids from Jewell Hill thought they were better than the kids from out in the county. If you didn't comb your hair a certain way, have the right shirt or jeans, or if you didn't have a car, you weren't with the in crowd. A lot of kids from the county dropped out of school. J. D. Marler and Mack Woody dropped out in the middle of the tenth grade.

I'd thought about dropping out. But I liked my history and English classes, especially Mrs. Slone and Mr. Bennett, who taught English. Mr. Bennett was interested in the words and expressions I'd use in class and in my compositions—things I'd learned from Grandma and Grandpa Smith. And I could tell of Grandma Smith's beliefs about bees and white spots under the fingernails, and what it meant for two people to get their hoes tangled in a row. I could sing the ballad of Lottie Yates and Little Margaret. Mr. Bennett didn't think it was stupid when I told that Grandma Smith said someone was "clever" when she meant they were generous. He said that was an old meaning of the word. He gave me the titles of some books to check out of the library—*Our Southern Highlanders* and *The Southern Highlander and His Homeland*. When I read these books I found a lot of things Grandma and Grandpa Smith said. I discovered we were southern Highlanders, and, just as Grandma Wells had said, most of our ancestors had come from England and Scotland, Ireland and Germany. Most had lived in Virginia and Pennsylvania before they came to Tennessee and other parts of southern Appalachia.

Appalachia was a word I learned from Mrs. Slone. She kidded us about not knowing where Appalachia was—

because we were sitting right in the middle of it, she said. She disagreed with Mr. Bennett on some things, but they were both interested in Appalachia. They let us write essays that counted for both English and history, and once they arranged to have their history and English classes meet together for a debate on strip-mining. It was no secret that they were both against it.

-»>> «<-

MOST BOYS FROM OUT in the county belonged to the Future Farmers of America club at West Madison, so I joined, too—before I knew about the initiation. It was coming up soon now, and I dreaded it. In fact, the night before the initiation was scheduled at school, about three weeks after I had begun my junior year, I got sick. Grandpa Smith asked me if I wanted to go fox hunting with him, but I begged off, I felt so tough. He got Eugene to go with him. Feeling guilty about having secretly set traps for foxes, dreading the FFA initiation next day, I lay awake and feverish, my thoughts rising off me in the dark like sparks that fly up when you stir a fire.

I wasn't sure whether it was really fever, or whether my own fear of the FFA initiation burned in me. I did know that at school next day I'd have a blindfold tied on me, I'd have to run a line of inch-thick paddles, grabble in a bucket of water for a fish that wasn't there, wearing a wire around my middle finger, while someone cranked an old wall telephone and shocked the stuffing out of me. I'd have to eat worms and beetles, stand with a hangman's noose around my neck, fall, still blindfolded, through the trapdoor, have my pecker painted green, and wear my clothes for three days wrong side out and backwards, an ear of corn swinging from a string around my neck—I'd heard all the awful details from the seniors.

I lay slipping in and out of dreams dark as the inside of a cow, dreams that glowed like Lloyd Sluder's blacksmith shop and hissed like red-hot horseshoes plunged into a water tank. I thought I heard Grandpa Smith's hounds running back on Horse Knob and remembered the traps I'd set back there in the bluff, and especially the one set among half-rotted, crisscrossed logs, in black woods dirt where I'd found fox tracks.

I promised myself I'd move the traps out of the bluff, give up trying to trap foxes, and try only for mink and muskrat in the creek. Then I fell into the dark hole of a dream, drifted in a boat through mist that curled and twisted like ghosts walking on black water. Next morning, when I rose early to run my traps, Mom said I'd called out in my sleep and talked crazy. She'd got up and given me two aspirin, but I didn't remember it. I felt queasy, as if the fish I'd have to feel for at the FFA initiation already swam in my stomach.

Carlene Cantrell's old blue Chevrolet came up the drive, and Mom gathered up her sweater and purse and went on to work. I ran my trapline in the bluff under Horse Knob. When I came to each trap (undisturbed for three days running), I sprung it, pulled up the stake, and dropped the trap in the burlap sack I was carrying.

As I slipped through the ironwood thicket, heading for the next-to-last trap, the one I'd set among crisscrossed logs where I'd seen fox tracks, I heard the trap's chain rattle, and the sound went through me like electricity. I started pushing through the thicket, tripped in a tangle of rusty barbed wire that had once been a fence, scrambled free on my hands and knees, then stopped when I saw a big dog lying across a log, my trap's chain stretched tight.

I glanced around at the rotting logs, all clawed and chewed, at the ground torn up in a circle around the staked trap. The dog, muddy from rolling on the ground, came off the log growling, and bared its long white teeth. "Luke! Luke, boy!" The dog was so muddy and bedraggled, at first I hadn't recognized Grandpa Smith's big Walker foxhound! Oh, Lord! Now I'd played hob!

I stood watching Luke twist around and gnaw at the trap that held his left hind foot by only one toe. Maybe I could get him out of the trap. He would only have a sore toe, I'd move the traps to the creek, and Grandpa Smith would never know. I eased toward Luke, careful not to make a sudden move.

"Here, Luke, boy." I moved closer, talking to the dog, until he had stopped growling. Luke whined; his tail even began to wag feebly. Still talking to him, I eased my hands down to the trap. But when I touched it, Luke yelped, his head shot out like a snake's, and I rolled over backward against a log, the vicious snap of his jaws just missing me.

I'd got hot climbing the ridge over into the bluff, and I'd taken my denim jacket off and put it in the burlap sack I carried. I took the jacket out of the sack and put it on—to protect my arms—and moved closer to Luke again. "You know me, Luke, you know me, boy." I was panting, and my hand trembled, but Luke let me touch him. Then I eased a hand down to the trap. Luke winced, whined. I pressed down on the trap's spring. The slippery trap twisted under my hand, Luke growled and whirled, snapping at me, and I sprang backward over the log.

I got up, sat down on the log, and tried to stop shaking. I had to get Luke out of that trap! Grandpa Smith would break a tobacco stick over my back if he found out I'd caught his Luke in a steel trap—even if the trap had only caught Luke's toe.

I took off my jacket. Holding it in both hands, I moved closer to Luke again. This time the dog was wary, and I couldn't get as close as before. When I started to bend down beside him, he tensed and growled. *Whoo!* I threw my jacket over Luke's head, locked it between my knees, muffling his growls, and reached down for the trap.

Luke gave a big jerk, wrenched his head free, and was all over me in a second. As I rolled away, Luke snapped my ankle. I scrambled behind the log and untied my shoe. Luke had bitten through the leather on both sides. I pulled down my sock; blood oozed.

I still thought I could get Luke out of the trap—if I could just cover his head and hold him down long enough. But I couldn't even get close to him anymore. As long as I talked to him, Luke lay whining, looking up. But if I moved close, he came up on his front legs growling. And it would soon be time for me to catch the bus to school.

I left Luke in the trap. I couldn't get him out, and I didn't dare tell Grandpa Smith. I caught the school bus with Eugene and Jeanette. I tried to swallow. I burned and shivered. Blindfolded for the FFA initiation, I ran the line of paddles (thwacked against sandbags); I heard put-on screams. Someone untied my shoestrings. I bent on order, got one solid whack, and stumbled on. I grabbled for the fish ("Try on this ring, boy"). The shock grabbed my hand like steel jaws. I jerked my hand back, but the jaws held on, and the shock ran up my arm and exploded like fireworks in my elbow.

While Luke lay caught in the hateful trap, I climbed the gallows, stumbling in my blindfold, stood on the trapdoor, felt it drop from under my feet, like a steel trap's pan, and fell—about a foot. I ate spaghetti and dried beans in a sauce of mustard and castor oil ("Eat these here worms"—"Give him some of these bugs and beetles, too"). I threw it up, and they fed it back to me.

I was still blindfolded and gagging when they led me behind the school shop ("Drop your pants!"—"Hey, Slick, don't cut it off!"). Cold and wet—that was the paint going on. It would be green.

All that time Grandpa Smith's foxhound, muddy and bedraggled, lay panting in my mind.

Again after school—I was wearing my shirt and pants wrong side out and backwards now—I tried, alone, to get Luke out of the trap. Luke bit me that time on the hand. I came back to the house, and as I passed the barn I stopped under the breezeway and stood listening. I could hear Grandpa Smith up in the loft shucking corn. I went on toward the house, whining a little like Luke.

When Mom got home from work, and after she, Grandma Smith, Eugene, and Jeanette had finished making fun of my wrong-side-out and backwards shirt and jeans, I caught Mom in the front room by herself and told her about Luke. "I didn't mean to do it," I said. "But Luke's still in the trap and I've tried twice and I can't get him out!"

"Then you go straight and tell your grandpa!" Mom said.

I shook my head. I couldn't do it.

"If you won't, I will!" she said, and got up from the chair where she'd been resting.

I turned back to the door. "No. I'll go." I hurried to the barn, wondering how I could tell Grandpa Smith what I'd done—after he'd asked me not to set traps in the woods, after he'd even gone with me to the creek and helped me find good places to trap mink and muskrats.

But Luke was still in the trap, and had been all day and part of last night. I had to tell.

I ran the rest of the way to the barn, climbed the ladder to the loft, and looked around. Dust floated in slanting bars of light that streamed in through cracks in the wall. From behind a great pile of cornshucks an ear of corn flew through the air, struck the side of the barn, and fell into the bin.

I stood on the ladder with my head in the loft and hollered, "Grandpa, you've got to come! Luke's in a trap!" Then I backed down the ladder and stood out under the shed watching as Grandpa Smith came down the ladder slowly, carefully, muttering, "Bobby, Bobby, Bobby!" He stood on the ground, turned, and stood looking at me there with my shirt and pants on wrong side out and backwards. I wondered what he was thinking under his black hat.

Grandpa Smith didn't say anything. He came past me, the cuffs of his overalls going *swarp, swarp*, and reached for his snake-headed walking stick leaning against the barn beside the feedroom door. "Where 'bouts is he?"

I told him.

"All right, let's go!"

Grandpa Smith stepped toward the woodyard and pumped his double-bitted ax from the chopping block. I fell in behind him, and we started up the hill above the barn. Grandpa climbed, using his walking stick, carrying his ax in the other hand.

"I tooted my horn for Luke this mornin', when he didn't

come home," he said, "and again a while ago. Been worried about that dog all day."

We went through the pines, crossed the fence, and walked on through oaks and poplars. Grandpa Smith stopped, and with two licks chopped down a slender dogwood with a fork toward the top. I watched him trim the dogwood until it had the Y-shape of a calf's yoke. I thought I saw what Grandpa Smith was going to do, and I could have kicked myself for not having thought of it.

We went on. When we got close to the trap, I got out ahead of Grandpa Smith and went ripping through the ironwoods. Grandpa Smith came on through and stood beside me, looking down at Luke, who was on his front legs growling, his lips curled back from meat-red gums and hooked fangs. I took a step toward Luke. "Maybe if—" I started to say.

"You stay back," Grandpa Smith said, "if you don't want to get eat alive."

I knew only too well that Luke would bite us if he could. But I stood back while Grandpa Smith waited his chance and then quickly pinned Luke's head down with the forked dogwood. He held Luke's head down with one hand and reached for the trap with the other. But Luke got his head out from under the yoke, leaped at Grandpa, and bit him on the forearm. "You scamp!" Grandpa Smith hissed.

"He bit me twice," I said. "Once on the ankle, and here on my hand."

"Stand over here!" Grandpa Smith said.

I stood where he pointed. He poised the yoke over Luke again, then brought it down on the dog, just behind his shoulder blades, and pinned him to the ground. This time he held the yoke with both hands. Straining, looking wild-eyed, he jerked his head toward me. "Now get the trap," he grunted.

I dived for the trap, pressed the spring with both hands. Luke seemed to know his foot was free; he stopped struggling. Grandpa eased the yoke off Luke and stepped back. Luke limped a couple of steps, stopped, and shook dirt into the leaves.

Breathing hard, Grandpa Smith stood watching. "I would've—laid a hundred dollar bill in your hand, Bobby, before I'd have had Luke's foot in a trap."

"It's just one toe; it's not his whole foot," I said.

"I told—asked you not to set—traps in these woods." Grandpa Smith was still puffing.

I went about a hundred yards on up into the woods, sprung the last trap, pulled the stake, and dropped it in the sack with the others. "I won't ever set traps in the woods again, I swear it," I said.

We came down the ridge together, hurt and bleeding. Luke had bitten Grandpa Smith through his jacket sleeve, but still Luke's long teeth had broken the skin on Grandpa's forearm. I walked behind Grandpa Smith and Luke. I was sixteen years old, and felt ridiculous and humiliated with my pants and shirt on wrong side out and backwards.

"Your mama know you got bit?" Grandpa Smith asked me.

"I didn't tell her."

"I wouldn't mention it, then, if I was you. She'd just be uneasy and tore up."

"It's not anything, anyway."

"We'll doctor ourselves," he said. "All three of us need it after this splatterment."

Out in the barn, where Mom and Grandma Smith couldn't see us, we did our doctoring.

Feeling like a snake shedding its skin, I wore my clothes to school next day wrong side out and backwards. I'd got an ear of corn out of the loft, and wore it on a string around my neck, as I was required to. I wore my pecker green. I sweated, shivered, tried to swallow. That afternoon Pleas Garrett, the bus driver, noticed how puny I looked; he felt my throat with his thumb and forefinger, said he thought I had mumps, and told me to stay home next day. He was right, I did have mumps, and I didn't have to go to school for days.

I helped Grandpa Smith doctor Luke—held Luke's muzzle while, with a little pair of scissors, Grandpa clipped the toe that hung by a thread of skin. He lectured me, laughed at me, and warned me of what would happen to me if my mumps fell. He told such horrible tales of boys whose "seed" swelled to the size of cantaloupes, I wasn't tempted to run or jump. Forbidden even to chop or saw for the sake of children sleeping in my seed, I lollygagged, loafed, felt snaky, and shed a scaly green skin.

⟫⟫ *27* ⟪⟪

O UR TOBACCO PLANT beds failed the spring of my junior year. Grandpa Smith sent word by me down to Grandpa Wells that we'd have to locate some plants somewhere before he could start making the tobacco crop.

Grandpa Wells said Willard Sexton had plenty of plants. He asked me to go down to Willard's with him and see if we could buy some. We threw some baskets in the back of Grandpa Wells's old blue farm truck. Grandpa Wells picked up two or three baskets with his one hand and tossed them in the back of the truck. I drove Grandpa Wells's truck so much now, I didn't even ask if I could drive. I just got in under the wheel, and he got in on the other side. I was comfortable driving trucks. I'd got my driver's license just before Christmas, driving Jess Barnes's log truck.

It was farther down to Sextons' by the road than it would have been just to walk across the fields. I remembered how, when I was eight or nine, and we'd come to Grandma Wells's on Sunday afternoons, I'd watch Velma Sexton through Grandpa Wells's binoculars.

Back then, I could see her down there on the porch, even without the binoculars. With them, I could bring Velma up so close I seemed to be standing there in the Sextons' yard, beside the porch; so close I used to feel that if I just called her name, she'd look up at me, like a dog whose name you call. Without the binoculars, I could see the color of her dress—white or blue—but with the glasses I could see that the dress was just an upside-down feed sack with holes cut for her arms.

She would be playing with a doll, or a bunch of sticks —and her a grown woman. Sometimes she would paddle the doll, or just sit gnawing on a stick. Through the binoculars I could see that her reddish hair was close-cropped. Sometimes her parents, Mr. and Mrs. Sexton, would come out on the porch and sit in rocking chairs. They never rocked, they just sat, and they didn't pay any attention to Velma, even when she gnawed on a stick, or beat her doll with a stick. They wouldn't move, except to swat a fly. Mr. and Mrs. Sexton both had white hair, like Grandma and Grandpa Wells.

I remembered Dad had said Velma had been as normal as the next person until she'd been afflicted. The Sextons had other children, some older than Velma, some younger, but they were all grown up and gone, except for Velma's brother, Willard, who lived at home and ran the farm, now that Mr. Sexton was too old to do much farm work.

Even after that I would sometimes take the binoculars outside and look around with them. Once or twice I walked up on the hill and sneaked a look at Velma. But as I grew older, the binoculars lost their fascination. When Dad would take us down to Grandma and Grandpa Wells's, after he and Mom separated, I became more interested in Grandpa Wells's horses, then in his tractor. And now I was interested in his truck, and his old green Hudson Hornet, which he'd been letting me drive some, but not on the highway.

Now that I had my driver's license, I wanted to ask Grandpa Wells if I could drive his Hudson that Friday night, to take Frieda Dean Rogers to our junior banquet, but I hadn't got up the nerve yet. I concentrated on driving his farm truck carefully, so I could point out what a good driver I was when I did ask. I'd really wanted to take Selma Austin, but Selma said she needed to study. Besides, she said, it was a banquet for juniors. She was only a freshman. I should ask a girl in my own class. I figured Selma just didn't want to go with me. But it was true that she studied a lot.

I drove carefully and thought about Velma, the woman-child. Although I didn't say a word about her, I wondered if we would see her while we were at Sextons'. Whenever I'd see her brother, Willard, at the store, I'd think about Velma and about how I used to watch her through Grandpa Wells's binoculars. But I had never been down the long drive to the Sextons' house.

No one was on the porch when we pulled up beside a tractor and parked. I climbed the porch steps behind Grandpa Wells. He stopped, opened the little gate with his one hand, and I closed it carefully while he knocked. Mr. Sexton came to the door. He was a handsome, white-haired old man with bright blue eyes and a ruddy face. He smiled when he recognized Grandpa Wells, and asked us into the living room, where Grandpa Wells and I sat on an old wicker sofa. Mr. Sexton sat across from us in a rocking chair, looking like a wise judge.

I knew Grandpa Wells wouldn't say anything about tobacco plants right away. That wasn't how you went about something like this. You visited first. You talked about everything else, and then, almost as an afterthought, you sidled up to the reason why you were there in the first place. I'd already been around with Grandpa Wells when he'd go to see people he wanted to help reelect him county magistrate, so I'd noticed how grown-ups did these things.

Grandpa Wells and Mr. Sexton talked easily about first one thing and another. Mr. Sexton seemed to know a lot about politics and things that were going on in the world. He fixed his blue eyes on me, smiled—his face was as warm as a fireplace—and allowed I was a fine-looking boy. Mrs. Sexton stepped in from the kitchen, holding a big wooden spoon, and inquired about Grandma Wells. She allowed I was a fine-looking boy, too, and would we stay for supper?

No, Grandpa Wells said, and thanked her just the same. We'd be getting on back home for supper. He said he wanted to talk to Willard—if Willard was home.

Willard had gone to turn some cattle into a new pasture field and should be home any time now, Mr. Sexton said.

While they went on talking, I sat there thinking how familiar Mr. and Mrs. Sexton were to me. They never left the place much. Once or twice I'd seen Mr. Sexton with Willard at Grandpa Wells's Trading Post. But I had never seen Mrs. Sexton, except at a distance, in her yard or garden. This was the first time I had ever been in their house, but they looked just like they used to when I'd watched them through Grandpa Wells's binoculars from the upstairs window.

Mrs. Sexton looked like all the grandmothers in the grade-school readers—plump and white-haired, with steel-rimmed glasses, an open, pleasant face, and a cheerful voice. Mr. Sexton was tall and lean, and appeared to be folded into the rocking chair across from us, his neat brown brogans planted flat on the floor. A well-fed calico cat came and rubbed against his leg, then sat as motionless as a book-end. Although he was friendly and hospitable and so obviously at ease in his chair, Mr. Sexton's long white head, curved nose, and keen blue eyes made me think of a hawk. If he'd put on a striped hat, he could have been Uncle Sam.

Mr. Sexton was talking about our Middle East policy when Willard came home. Flashing a gold tooth at me and Grandpa Wells, Willard took off his feedstore hat, hung it on the post of a straight-backed, split-bottom chair, and sat down with his big brown hands on his knees. Willard was tall and lean like his father.

The talk turned to cattle for a few minutes. Then, when Grandpa Wells brought up the subject of blue mold, I knew he was getting around to buying some tobacco plants. Yes, a lot of plant beds had failed and put so many folks in a bind; it was—

I would not have been more surprised if, in the next moment, a tree had come crashing into the living room of the Sextons' house and fallen across my legs. All I saw was a blur of white, and then something hit me, landed in my lap, and locked onto me. I drew back, as best I could on the wicker sofa, and knew I was looking into the face of Velma. She had come from somewhere, leaped onto my lap, and grabbed my arms at the biceps. I was looking right into her face, feeling her hot breath, and I could see she had bad teeth and several hairs on her chin, tough and black as hog bristles.

"Come down from therre!" Mr. Sexton said, in the drawn-out gutteral manner Grandpa Smith used when he ordered a dog off the porch.

"I said doowwn!" Mr. Sexton repeated. All the friendliness had gone out of his ruddy face. Looking more hawklike than ever, he picked up a flyswatter, half-rose from his rocker, and whacked Velma across the forearm.

Velma gripped my arms tighter, cocked her head, and looked at me with eyes a soapstone blue. Her hair, which had been reddish years ago when I'd watched her through the binoculars, was still close-cropped, but now it was as gray as steel wool.

"Willard, get her off the boy!" Mr. Sexton said.

Willard grabbed Velma's arm and jerked her free of me. She flew sideways off my lap, scraped over the edge of the wicker sofa, and when she hit the flowered linoleum—hard, her legs folded beneath her—she slid on it. The calico cat sprang behind the black woodstove. I saw that Velma's white shift really was, as I had used to think, an inverted feedsack with holes cut in the bottom corners for her arms.

She lay there a minute, then raised her head. Her face was dried and shriveled, with dark splotches and whorls, like a cured smokehouse ham. She looked up at Willard, crawled on her hands and knees toward him, grabbed his legs with both arms, and, turning to Mrs. Sexton, said, *"Mama, can I seep wiz Wiw-ad tonight?"*

"Put her in the back room, Willard," Mr. Sexton said. He had sat back down in his rocker, with his flyswatter across

his knees. He seemed calmer now, as if our neighborly conversation had been interrupted by the cat overturning a dish of cream.

Willard half-dragged, half-carried his resisting sister out of the living room. I heard him talking to her in that way men talked to dumb animals, but all I could hear was: "*Git . . . now . . . Over there!*" Velma said "*Wiw-ad*" three or four times. A door slammed. Willard came back in and sat down, brushing his pants legs smooth, as if he had just disposed of a messy business. Yeah, he said, there were just lots of folks didn't have plants this year, and tobacco-setting time was on us.

Grandpa Wells reached over and grabbed my knee and massaged it slowly. He said that was what he'd come to see Willard about. We needed plants in the worst way and hoped Willard would sell him enough to set out our allotment.

Willard nodded, and rubbed a forefinger along his nose. He had been getting inquiries about plants all the way from North Carolina and Georgia. People's plant beds had failed everywhere, it looked like. But he thought a man ought to help out his neighbors first—do for them, if he could. He was just glad he had such fine plant beds this year.

Willard took his hat off the back of his straight-backed chair. He invited Grandpa Wells and me to come out to his plant beds and he'd show us what he could spare.

We walked out beyond the big black barn to the tobacco beds. Grandpa Wells said they were surely fine plants. He said every green leaf looked like a dollar bill to him. Grandpa Wells cut a deal with Willard right there.

Grandpa Wells told me to go get the truck and drive it out past the barn to the plant beds. We'd pull plants till we filled up the baskets we'd brought, he said, or until it got dark, whichever came first.

Willard offered to help us pull plants, but Grandpa Wells said, "No, you go on to the house and eat your supper, Willard." He said he didn't expect Willard to accommodate us this way, and then have to help us pull the plants, too. Willard said he was just glad he had plants to spare. Grandpa Wells said he was much obliged to Willard.

While Willard went on to supper, Grandpa Wells and I pulled plants and put them in the baskets, clumps of dark soil still clinging to their roots.

Willard was a good neighbor, Grandpa Wells said.

I said he sure was.

We were down on our knees at the lower end of the plant bed, reaching over into it, pulling plants. Grandpa Wells had only the one hand to pull plants with, but still he pulled as many as I did.

Willard could have sold these plants for twice what he let us have them for, Grandpa Wells said.

I said I guessed he could have.

We were quiet a long time. The only sounds were the muffled snapping of the plant roots as we pulled plants from the bed.

Then Grandpa Wells said, "She didn't hurt you, did she? Velma?"

"Nah!"

I put a handful of plants into a basket and added, "Scared the livin' fire out of me, though!"

Grandpa Wells said he figured Velma had scared me. He said when she jumped on me, I'd turned right white around the mouth.

"She's stout, too!" I said.

"And quick as a mink!" Grandpa Wells said. He said he didn't see her until she was astraddle me.

I said I hadn't seen her, either.

We didn't say anything for a while. Then Grandpa Wells said the Sextons were fine people, and it was a pity about Velma. Always had been. A pity. The Sextons could have put Velma away, years ago, but they thought she'd be better off at home.

Again we pulled plants in silence. After a while Grandpa Wells said, "Pay no attention to what Velma said—about sleeping in Willard's bed. In her mind, she's just a child. You understand that, don't you?"

Could he have read my mind and known that as I was kneeling there beside him, pulling tobacco plants, I was wondering if Velma really did sleep in Willard's bed? But I knew Grandpa Wells was right, so I said yes, I understood.

"Willard ought not to have jerked her down that way, as hard as he did," Grandpa said. "Hard to meddle in a thing like that, though."

I finished filling up a basket and carried it to the truck. I was glad we'd brought Grandpa Wells's farm truck, and not his car. If we'd hauled baskets of tobacco plants home in it, I'd have had to clean it up good before I took Frieda Dean Rogers to the junior class banquet in it. Of course, I didn't know if Grandpa Wells would let me borrow his car. And I'd kept putting off asking him, afraid he'd say no.

But somehow—I didn't know exactly why—now seemed like a good time to ask. So back at the plant bed, kneeling beside him, I asked.

Frieda Dean Rogers. Was that one of Clayton Rogers's girls? Grandpa Wells asked.

"Yes." I held my breath.

"Clayton's got a passel of girls."

"Five," I said. "And they've got a baby brother, three years old."

"Old Clayton. Well, he always votes right. They tell he said he'd have a boy, or else fill the holler full of girls. Maybe he can be satisfied now. Nice girl, is she?"

"Sure. She's in my class."

"Clayton, he's a cousin to Walter Lee Rogers, I believe. You know Walter Lee, don't you?"

Grandpa Wells was kidding now. He knew I knew Walter Lee Rogers. "He's Mom's boyfriend," I said.

"You think they'll eventually marry?" Grandpa Wells asked.

"I think Mom would," I said. "If he ever asked her to. But Walter Lee's so slow. After he wanted to ask Mom for a date, he waited six months before he got around to it. Anyway, that's what Mom said."

Grandpa Wells grinned. He said I'd better be careful, because if Walter Lee and Mom got married, and if I was to get thick with Frieda Dean Rogers, I might end up being my own grandpa!

"I'm just taking her to the junior class banquet!" I said.

Grandpa Wells asked if I knew to treat these girls right when I took them out places.

I wanted to say something indignant, like, What did he mean by that? Instead, I said, "Sure." I didn't want to risk reversing what was sounding more and more like a yes answer. Besides, I suspected he said that because he was still thinking about the way Willard had jerked Velma off me.

We pulled plants till dark, carried more baskets of plants and set them in the back of the truck, and I drove us home.

I thought about how I might just clean up Grandpa's car some more, anyway.

As I turned out of the Sextons' drive onto the road, I realized this was the first time I had ever driven at night. By the time I pulled in up at Grandpa Wells's, it seemed to me that I had been driving after dark for years.

⋙ 28 ⋘

I GUESS I DIDN'T spend more than two or three days at home the summer between my junior and senior years at West Madison. I helped George Hawkins haul watermelons from Florida and Georgia. Sometimes I'd get out to Newfound just to pick up clean clothes. Going to sleep by a swamp in Florida, or under a live-oak tree in south Georgia, or loading watermelons at night on a farm where the bitter fragrance of flu-cured tobacco hung on the evening air, I'd think of Newfound Creek and Grandma and Grandpa Smith, Mom and Dad, Jeanette and Eugene, and they would all seem far away, as if they were part of another life I'd lived long ago. I was homesick a little, but when I was, I thought mostly about Selma Austin. When I was a couple of days selling out a load of watermelons at the farmer's market in Mountain City, I'd go by and see Dad, if he happened to be in his office. But mostly I'd lie in the straw in the back of George Hawkins's truck, wait for customers, and listen to country music from the restaurant opposite the market there on Lexington Avenue. Then I thought a lot about Selma.

That summer ended and I started my last year of school. Chinquapins ripened early. On the first Saturday morning after school began, the big prickly burrs on the chinquapin bushes had already turned yellow and burst open, and the chinquapins were shiny black in the morning sunlight. A storm had passed through in the night, but now the air was clear and the mountains seemed to have moved closer. I picked two pockets full of them on the ridge above Grandpa Smith's barn and then walked down the Newfound Creek road toward Austins', hoping to see Selma.

She was sitting at a wooden table under the sycamore tree in the yard, in one of the woven willow chairs the Sutherlands had made, wearing jeans and a pullover, glancing first at an open book, then writing in her notebook. Her little brother Charles Everett crawled about in his playpen at the end of the table. I stepped in behind the big oak tree at the edge of the yard and lobbed a chinquapin at Selma. It bounced on the table beside her; she looked up in the sycamore tree, then started writing again. I lobbed another chinquapin that popped right on the page she was writing on. She looked around. Maybe she saw me draw my arm back. "All right, Robert Wells," she said. "I know you're behind that tree."

I crossed the yard, dragging my feet through the big, crackly sycamore leaves that had already fallen, and sat down at the table beside her. She looked warm and snug in the woolly pullover; her movements as she glanced first at her literature textbook, then at her notebook, were small and quick, like a bird's.

"Sleepyhead, where were you at seven?" I asked.

"I was up at seven, eating breakfast," she said, and went on writing. Selma had a reputation at school for working hard and being smart. If she kept on making good grades, she was sure to get a scholarship to a college.

"I was up, too, but I didn't see you," I said. I'd driven down the road in Grandpa Wells's old farm truck that morning, hauling corn to Tom Davis's mill to be crushed for Grandpa Wells's cattle. I told Selma I'd driven by, trying to sound as if it were something I did every day of my life. The truth was, I hauled the corn just to get to drive Grandpa Wells's truck.

"Did Eugene go with you?" Selma asked. She smiled brightly at Charles Everett, who had pulled up to a standing position and was shaking his playpen violently and babbling, trying to attract her attention. Selma cooed to him.

"No, Eugene's at the house. But he's the only one. Mom and Grandpa and Grandma Smith and Jeanette went to Jewell Hill. They all rode with Carlene Cantrell." I saw the little blue veins in the back of Selma's pretty, smooth hands, and noticed the way her fingers gripped the pencil as she wrote. I had always noticed Selma's hands.

"Tell Eugene not to forget to bring me my history book," she said.

I made the sound of galloping horses on the table with my fingers, and felt disgusted. I had so many tender, heroic things to say to Selma, yet everything came out silly and stupid, like my telling her about hauling corn to mill, while she did her lessons and cooed to her little brother, or worried about her history book. "You want some chinquapins?" I asked.

"No, thanks. They make my tongue sore."

I took hold of the rubber band on her wrist, stretched it, and let it snap back.

"Ouch! Stop that!"

I knew what I was doing was just another stupid thing, but I couldn't keep from doing it. I stretched the rubber band again.

Selma twisted her body around, grabbed my arm with her hand, and dug her sharp fingernails into my wrist. "You'd better let go," she said, her voice rising in warning.

I held on to the rubber band, threatening to let it snap against her wrist.

"All right!" she said, sinking her fingernails deeper, really hurting. Her lips were pressed tightly together, her eyes almost shut, she was gripping so hard.

I drew my arm close to me, and her with it, until she was against me, her lips close to mine, her eyes half-closed. She gasped; I felt her warm breath on my lips. Then she let go of my wrist and I quickly slipped the rubber band off her arm.

"Devil!" she said, patting her brown hair with both hands.

"Devil yourself!" I said, and showed her the deep red crescents her fingernails had made in my wrist. "You ought to be ashamed," I teased. I was very happy at that moment.

"Well, bless his little arm!" she said with mock tenderness, and took my hand gently in both of hers. She raised my obedient hand toward her lips, as if to kiss the red crescents; then, with a diabolical giggle, she cut deep into my wrist with her fingernails again. The deception hurt more than her fingernails.

"Charles Everett, you stop that!" she said, turning from me. Her little brother, down on his hands and knees in the playpen, had reached out through the bars and got a fistful of dried grass and was trying to eat it. Selma smacked his hand, took the grass away from him, and set him in the center of the playpen. "Here, little dirt-dauber, play with your spools."

I picked up one of the spools, cut notches on both ends with my knife, then cut a couple of little twigs from a low-hanging limb, and with the spool, the twigs, and the rubber band, I made Selma's little brother a tractor. I wound it up, set it on the floor of the playpen, and let it creep toward him. He sat very still watching it. "Tractor," I said. Charles Everett waved his arms excitedly and tried to say tractor.

I wound the tractor again, turned to Selma, and put it down on her shoulder. The tractor started creeping on the woolly green pullover. She drew her head down, turning to Charles Everett. "Make him stop, Charles Everett. Robert is a bigger baby than you are." Her little brother waved his arms and babbled. She wound the tractor up, set it down in his playpen, and picked up her pencil again.

Suddenly I realized that Selma surely knew I didn't come by to sit in the yard with her because I liked to flip rubber bands or make spool tractors for her little brother. Maybe she didn't know how I had thought about her all summer, in Florida, in Georgia, in South Carolina, but surely she must know I liked her, loved her. "I have to write an essay," I sighed, watching her write.

"What on?"

"Love," I lied. Actually, Mr. Bennett, my English teacher, had said we could write about anything that had happened to us during the summer, or about anything we thought was worth writing about.

Selma bent down again to wind the tractor for Charles

Everett. I disliked her little brother. Every time I came to the brink of saying something to Selma that I really wanted to say—not just stupid, silly stuff—her little brother did something to distract her. I threw a chinquapin against the oak tree—so hard the chinquapin bounded halfway back into the yard. "I'd better go get started on that essay," I said, and walked off through the noisy leaves.

"Tell Eugene when he's through with my—"

"Yeah, I will." I walked away, throwing chinquapins high into the deep, blue sky, remembering painfully how Selma had started to kiss my wrist, then dug in with her fingernails.

I came around the side of the hill, through the stubby lespedeza, and stopped at the corner of the barn when I saw Eugene standing on the kitchen porch, stripped to the waist, his back to me. For a minute I couldn't figure what he was doing. Then I saw the aluminum pan on the work-table and the towel hanging over the edge of the table. Eugene was shaving—or trying to. He was looking into the mirror and the reflection of the razor was confusing him, for he kept changing his grip on it, trying to discover the right way to hold it.

I started to turn away, for I didn't want Eugene to think I had been standing there watching him shave for the first time—although that was exactly what I had been doing. He must have felt my presence, because he turned, his face covered with so much lather he looked like Santa Claus, and saw me. I came on into the backyard and climbed the steps up to the kitchen porch, trying to act as if Eugene were doing the most ordinary thing in the world.

"Lots of chinquapins this year," I said. "I got my pockets full in a few minutes."

Eugene pinched the tip of his nose and carefully shaved his upper lip. The razor didn't make a sound. "That so?" he said when he had finished with his upper lip.

I went on talking about chinquapins, telling him where every chinquapin bush in the whole county was, while Eugene said he knew, or didn't know, where those bushes were, or else he just grunted. I guess he must have thought I was crazy to stand there for fifteen minutes and talk about nothing but chinquapins. All I was trying to do was keep him from being embarrassed by standing there, without saying something smart about his shaving for the first time.

He finished, splashed water on his face, and dried with the towel. I glanced secretly at his face, and it was as if I had never seen him before. Eugene was fifteen now, and his face was strangely different; and yet it was the same difference I had often noticed in boys' faces. I wouldn't see them all summer, and then when I saw them again after school started in the fall, they'd be different. I guess the same thing had happened to me, but I hadn't noticed it about myself.

I hadn't seen Eugene all summer, and now it had happened to him. The baby roundness of his face had hardened into definite planes and angles; his jaw was firmer, his nose more prominent and slightly curved, instead of just being a button. In that secret glance that caught only the outline of his face, I saw the change, saw what he would look like as a man. I looked more closely, and the difference seemed to fade, then come again. I thought Eugene looked a little like the faces of our people in the oval picture frames down at Grandma and Grandpa Wells's and on the wall here at Grandma and Grandpa Smith's.

"Have some chinquapins," I said quickly, when I became aware that I was staring at him. I gave him a handful. Now Eugene looked like the face in the old tintype, the one Grandma Smith found behind the picture of our great-grandfather Leland.

"Thanks. Maybe I'll go up on the ridge this afternoon and pick some, too. Pay you back."

I followed Eugene through the kitchen and back to our room, where I got Mom's little portable typewriter, the one she had practiced at home with. I carried the typewriter out to the porch, where I sat down to write my essay. I sat a long time trying to decide what to write about. There were so many things. I could write about all the trips I'd made hauling watermelons that summer. But all I could think of was Eugene's face, and Selma, sitting at the table in her yard, studying and babysitting her little brother. I wondered if she would still be there when I drove past later in the afternoon, bringing the crushed corn from the mill in Grandpa Wells's old farm truck. Then I remembered the Sutherlands and decided to write about them. I wrote a while, went into the kitchen and made a sandwich, came back out on the porch, and went on writing.

It was almost two o'clock, and I was retyping my essay when Eugene came out on the porch. He had already been up on the ridge picking chinquapins, and he had both pockets full. He stood on the porch a minute, then went back into the house; I heard him pulling out drawers and slamming them shut again. A minute later he came out on the kitchen porch and asked me if I knew where Mom kept her needles. I told him. He went back inside, clomped out a few minutes later, and stood with his thumbs hooked in the top of his beltless jeans, watching me type. "Can I have a piece of fishing line off your reel?"

"How much?"

"Not much. Just a little. Two feet?"

"Sure. What do you want it for?"

"I need a piece." He went back inside.

I finished copying what I had written and took my notebook back to our room. I tried to open the door, but it was latched from the inside. Eugene came to the door and unlatched it. I put my notebook down and started back out. Eugene was tinkering with the lock. "Must be something wrong with it," he said, turning the knob back and forth. He popped a chinquapin into his mouth.

"Selma said for you to bring her her history book when you're through with it."

Eugene snapped his fingers, chewed a minute. He picked up the book and fell across the bed with it. "I've not even started to read it," he said.

I paused in the door, not knowing where to go or what to do. I had the feeling there was something I had intended to say to Eugene, but I must have forgotten it. I went down and waited on the porch. It was very quiet with Mom, Jeanette, and Grandma and Grandpa Smith gone to Jewell Hill with Carlene Cantrell, and Eugene lying on the bed reading. The whole day had been strange: first, walking down to Grandpa Wells's in the early morning chill and hauling corn to mill in his truck; then picking chinquapins on the ridge and sitting with Selma; noticing Eugene's face; and now this stillness, the deep blue sky, bright sun, the puffs of milkweed floating through the air, and the rustling of leaves in the trees in the yard when a breeze stirred—like a far-off waterfall. It seemed that everything was changing; everything stayed a little while, then passed on, like Newfound School, or the Sutherlands, or bees that decided, mysteriously, to leave a hive and fly away in a dark cloud.

Carlene brought Mom, Jeanette, and Grandma and Grandpa Smith home about three-thirty. (Mom still hadn't learned to drive.) I helped them carry shopping bags into the house. Grandpa Smith had bought two bales of barbed wire. We lifted them carefully out of the trunk of Carlene Cantrell's old Chevrolet, then carried them to the barn by running a crowbar through the hole in the bale.

Later I walked back down to Grandpa Wells's, got his truck, and drove to the mill to pick up the sacks of crushed corn. I drove slowly along the dusty gravel road. When I got to the mill, Tom Davis, the miller, his ears white with cornmeal dust, shouted to me over the roar of the mill that my sacks wouldn't be ready for at least an hour. I paced up and down in front of the mill. But there was no way to hurry Tom Davis. I got in Grandpa Wells's truck and drove over to the old blacksmith shop, where I'd seen some cars parked as I'd come down the road. J. D. Marler, Mack Woody, and some more boys were playing blackjack for pennies. I played for a while and lost all the pennies I had.

It was after five when I got the sacks loaded and started back with them. Selma probably wouldn't be out in the yard this late. But she might be. No, she probably wouldn't be. I whipped around the turn: she was. And Eugene had come to bring her history book. I turned off the road and pulled down the Austins' drive, cut the switch at the edge of the yard, and walked across to where they were sitting at the table under the sycamore tree.

Selma had brought out cake and milk for her and Eugene; they were sitting at the table nibbling cake, their heads together over the history book. "Hi," Selma said, without looking up. I stood behind them and peered over Eugene's shoulder, pretending to look at the open book. But I was really looking at the chinquapin necklace Selma was wearing—the kind Jeanette always made. I stood there behind Selma and Eugene, and saw that the chinquapins were strung on my black fishing line.

"What did you say for number fourteen?" Selma asked Eugene.

I popped a chinquapin into my mouth, cracked it open, and stood there pushing the meaty center out of the hull with the tip of my tongue. Selma's little brother Charles Everett threw his spool tractor out of the playpen, then reached through the bars for it, but it was too far away. He gathered a fistful of dry grass; very carefully and thoughtfully he began stuffing the grass into his mouth. Selma didn't even notice.

⇛ 29 ⇚

S OON AFTER I BEGAN my senior year at West Madison
I got a big brown envelope from Aunt Vi. The
envelope had a lot of papers and brochures in it,
and a letter from Aunt Vi written on the letterhead of the
college where she taught in Pennsylvania. At first I thought
she was saying I should come to her college. But she was
explaining about a college in Kentucky, where I could go
to school even though I didn't have much money. At Berea
College, students could work to pay for all their school
expenses. The envelope full of papers and brochures explained all about Berea College. One of the places where
students could work was Fireside Industries. That sounded
cozy.

I showed Grandma Wells the things Aunt Vi had sent
me. She smiled. Yes, by all means, I should apply,
Grandma Wells said, for it would be a wonderful opportunity. She added that she had asked Aunt Vi to see that
the materials about Berea College were sent to me.

In Mountain City—I rode there with Grandpa Wells—

I went by Dad's office and told him about Berea College. He made a quick telephone call and we went to lunch in a nearby restaurant. A pretty blond woman came and sat down at the table with us. Dad introduced us. Her name was Flora, and she smiled and smelled good. While we ate, she talked to Dad and kept putting her hand on his. I thought about her name—Flora. It rhymed with Mom's name—Nora.

Dad told Flora I was thinking about going to college. He showed Flora the brochures. He had gone to Sevier College before he quit, but he knew about Berea College, and he agreed with Grandma Wells that I should apply. Flora thought I should apply, too. Outside the restaurant she kissed Dad on the cheek and gave me a hug.

"That's Flora—Flora Addington," Dad said as we walked back to his office. "I wanted you to meet her."

I figured it had been Flora he had called just before we left his office.

"Did you like her?" Dad asked.

He was trying to tell me Flora was his girlfriend, but I knew that just by the way she came in and sat down with us. I said I liked her fine. Dad said he did, too.

"Mom has a boyfriend," I said.

"Old Walter Lee," Dad said. "How do you like him?"

I said I liked him fine. Grandma and Grandpa Smith liked Walter Lee, too. When he came by to see Mom, Walter Lee would talk to Grandma about his folks, and then to Grandpa about fox hunting. Walter Lee and Mom looked funny together because he was so much taller. He had gray hair in his sideburns, but from the back he sometimes looked like a knot-headed boy. "His ears stick out," Eugene said once. "Looks like he's about to fly."

"Hush!" Mom said. She said Walter Lee might look like he was about to fly, but she had never known anybody who had his feet more solidly on the ground than he did.

Walter Lee carried a big wallet in his hip pocket. A plaited leather thong connected the wallet to his belt. Jeanette asked Mom if she knew how much money Walter Lee had in his wallet. She bet he had a thousand dollars in it.

Mom grinned. She didn't know, but however much it was, she bet the first dollar Walter Lee ever made was in there. Walter Lee was as close as he was slow, Mom said.

"Nothing wrong with being close," Grandma Smith said. Anyway, all the Rogerses were saving.

Walter Lee was always saying funny things and making Jeanette laugh. He made Jeanette laugh even when she felt bad. Once when Walter Lee came by to see Mom, Jeanette had had a shot at school and felt grumpy. She wouldn't laugh at anything Walter Lee said—until Walter Lee was telling Mom he'd just bought his new hunting license. He winked at Jeanette, showed her the new license, and said it was his vaccination against game wardens.

→≫ ≪←

MRS. SIMPSON, THE COUNSELOR at West Madison, gave me some tests Berea College sent her. I filled out the application forms and wrote an essay about why I wanted to attend Berea College. Early in the spring I got a letter saying I was accepted. As soon as I read the letter, I began to leave Newfound Creek and my family. I read and reread all the papers and brochures and catalogues Berea College sent me, studied the pictures, and imagined what it would be like in Kentucky. I got some books out of the library and read more about Kentucky. I got a map and figured out the route from Newfound Creek to Berea College. I knew what the map said, I knew it was where Mom and Dad had gone to get married, but in my mind college lay up ahead, a country where everyone spoke a foreign language.

· "Reckon what kind of country it is up there in Kentucky?" Grandpa Smith wondered one evening after supper. We were all sitting out under the maples. A bobwhite was calling from the orchard grass below the barn.

I said I'd be finding out and I'd tell him the first time I came home.

"They have horses," Jeanette said. "And the grass is blue."

"It is not," Eugene said. "Bluegrass is just the name of it. Clifford Shelton has got bluegrass in his pasture, and it's not blue. It's green like any other grass."

"I was only kidding, dopey," Jeanette said.

Grandma Smith said she'd always heard that some of her people went to Kentucky, back years ago, but she didn't know where they settled.

Mom said she thought Uncle Clinton knew; he'd had a letter from a Ponder in Kentucky.

I thought of the man in the dim tintype behind Great-grandfather Leland's picture, on the wall inside the house.

The bobwhite called again from below the barn.

Grandma Smith said they would all miss me.

"I'm not gone yet, Grandma," I said.

But I was gone, in my mind. The winter had been mild, we didn't miss any days because of snow, and so graduation came in late May. I was astonished to learn that I was salutatorian, with the second-highest grade average in my class. Before I gave my speech, Mr. Bennett said a few words about West Madison Consolidated High School and about the value of preserving traditions of the smaller schools we students had attended before West Madison brought us all together. In the smaller schools students had been encouraged to tell stories and present recitations before their schoolmates. Mr. Bennett thought this was a tradition worth preserving and he encouraged storytelling and public speaking at West Madison. Then he introduced me as a graduate who had come from the Newfound School to West Madison.

I gave a speech called "Citizens of Somewhere." Mr. Bennett and Mrs. Slone had read it twice and made corrections and suggestions. I told how, when I knew I would be going to college, Grandma Smith had said so many young people from Newfound left home after school and became "citizens of nowhere." I talked about the hundreds of thousands of people who had left our Appalachian region over the years to seek work in other places. I asked why we had to leave a place that was so beautiful; why the natural beauty that attracted tourists from all over the country was being destroyed, in many places, by strip-mining. I recited a poem that Mr. Bennett had read to us, a poem called "Heritage," that described the hills toppling their heads to level earth and forests sliding out of the sky. I talked about the Sutherlands and the baskets and chairs they made, about old-fashioned ways and modern ways, about mules and missiles. I said I thought I was somebody from somewhere, from a place I would be leaving to attend college, but hoped to return to.

My whole family was in the audience—Mom with Walter Lee Rogers, Dad with Flora Addington, Eugene and Jeanette sitting with Grandma and Grandpa Smith and Grandma and Grandpa Wells. I watched them while I spoke and thought especially of Grandpa Wells, who had not much favored the idea when he'd first heard I would be going off to college. He'd wanted me to think about staying and helping him run the farm and store. But Grandma Wells had put a stop to that talk. And after graduation Grandpa Wells shook my hand and said I had "spizzerinctum." Dad said my speech was *almost* as good as the one he'd given the time he won the medal. Grandma Wells said she would be hard pressed to say which was better, for they were both good talks.

I HELPED GEORGE HAWKINS haul watermelons again that summer, and spent most of the time coming and going from Mountain City to Florida, Georgia, and South Carolina. I saved the money George paid me, and thought about how soon I would be going north to Berea College.

I would come home to Newfound Creek for a day or an evening, before we'd head south for another load, and catch up on the news. Home from one trip, I learned that Eugene was working in timber and saving his money to buy a car. When I came home another time, Eugene had already bought the car—a Mercury convertible—and he and Selma Austin had been to Jewell Hill to the drive-in. I was really surprised when I came home about a week after that and found out that now Eugene was teaching Mom to drive. She drove Eugene's car out to the barn, turned, and came back to the house while we all stood in the yard watching her. Jeanette and I clapped when she set the emergency brake carefully and got out. Grandpa Smith just stood with a funny little smile on his face. He said mountain people just naturally knew always to set the emergency brake when they got out of their cars.

I was home one Saturday in July when Jeanette came running up the road from Grandma and Grandpa Wells's. Jeanette was working three days a week now for Grandma Wells. She came huffing into the kitchen—I was drinking coffee, Mom was stirring cake batter—and held out a carpenter's level to Mom.

"Grandpa Wells said to give this to you," Jeanette said, still breathing hard. "He said you'd understand. I hope you do, because I don't!"

Mom set down the cake batter and, looking puzzled, took the level from Jeanette. "Where did this come from?" she asked.

Jeanette said Grandpa Wells and Willard Sexton had torn away the old porch steps that morning and were building new ones. Grandpa Wells had found the level under the old steps. He'd called Jeanette from her cleaning in the house and told her to take the level straight to Mom.

Mom just stood there holding the level with a look of great satisfaction on her face. "That's the level!" Mom said, looking first at me, then at Jeanette. "The very level!"

Then I remembered.

"That's the level your grandma Wells said I lost!" Mom said. "And Papa believed it, too, and whipped me." Mom kept standing there turning the level over and over in her hands.

Jeanette had to go back down to Grandma and Grandpa Wells's to finish cleaning.

"You tell Mr. Wells I understand," Mom said, "and say I thank him. Mr. Wells never did believe I lost that level," she said to me. "He said it didn't make any difference if I did."

When Grandma Smith came in from the barn with a basket of eggs, Mom showed her the level and retold the whole story. "I'll declare!" Grandma Smith said. Mom sent me down to the tobacco patch, where Grandpa Smith and Eugene were pulling suckers from the tobacco, to fetch Grandpa Smith to the house. Grandpa Smith didn't remember the level, so Mom reminded him of how, years ago, he'd switched her for losing it.

Grandpa Smith grinned and cocked his head to one side, like a bird. "And this level was under the steps all that time?" he asked.

Yes, Mom said, and Grandpa was actually the one who'd lost it, by building the steps around it.

Grandpa Smith said he was sorry he'd switched her legs and ankles for losing the level. He figured that must have been thirty years ago.

"That's right," Mom said. "I wasn't more than four or five years old." But the way she talked about it made it seem like only yesterday. She sat in the living room, her legs crossed, holding the level across her lap.

"One time you whipped me for something Robert did," Eugene told Mom.

"Is this your cake you've started?" Grandma Smith said from the kitchen.

Mom seemed not to hear either of them. Wiggling her foot contentedly inside her shoe, she said, "I knew all the time I never lost that level."

"What are you going to do with it?" Eugene said.

Mom said, "I think I'll frame it!"

I HAD PLANNED to get Eugene to drive me to Jewell Hill in his Mercury and then catch the bus from there to Berea College. But when I got to talking about it with George Hawkins, he said, "Pshaw, I'll drive you up there." George said he'd like to see what the country looked like up that way. So at five o'clock one morning in September George came to the house in his truck, the same one I'd ridden in two summers hauling watermelons. George always liked to get an early start, and since he didn't believe there was better water than what he had at home, he always brought his own jug of water.

Everyone had been up since four, knowing I was leaving early. I joked with Mom. "Hold it in the road!" I said to her. I hugged Jeanette, who was sitting in her gown, trying to keep her eyes open. "Go back to bed!" I told her. I shook Eugene's hand and told him to try to watch the movie at the drive-in. I hugged Grandma Smith and put my arm around Grandpa Smith. Out on the porch, where I picked up the suitcases Dad had bought for me in Mountain City, tears came in my eyes. I fumbled with the suitcases until I got hold of myself, then carried them to the truck that waited, idling, with all its amber running lights glowing in the thinning darkness. Still, I wasn't ready to go. I went to the dog lot in the stand of pines and said goodbye to my foxhound, Lady. I kissed her right on her cold nose.

⇶ ⇷

I wrote home and told what George Hawkins had said when we got to Berea. He looked all around, his hands jammed in his pockets, and said, "They've got more sky up here!" I wrote again to tell Grandpa Smith what I'd found out about squirrels. "Remember you told me once about hunting back on the Bearwallow and all these squirrels, hundreds of them, came past you, leaping through the trees?" I said I never had believed that story, but I had read in a magazine that zoologists from the Smithsonian Institution's Center for Short-lived Phenomena were hurrying to the Appalachian Mountains, where large numbers of squirrels were on the move. These scientists were observing gray squirrels crossing highways, scurrying across fields, swimming lakes. They were trying to figure out what caused these mass movements of squirrels, but as yet they didn't understand. I told Grandpa I believed him now. Mom answered for Grandpa on her typewriter. She said all Grandpa said was, "It happened."

I wrote letters to Eugene and Jeanette. Eugene didn't write back. Instead, he asked Jeanette to include his news in her letter: Mom was getting better and better at driving. He was teaching her to parallel park. He had taken Mom out on the Newfound Creek road to practice, but she was afraid of the curves; she wanted to stop the car, get out, and look around the curve to see if a car was coming before she drove on. Jeanette said she was pretty sure Mom and Walter Lee Rogers were going to get married. Because Walter Lee was Mom's boss at Blue Ridge Manufacturing, Jeanette had thought Mom probably didn't have to work hard, but Mom had said she had to work harder because she worked for Walter Lee. Jeanette was already thinking about having a bridal shower for Mom when they got married. That would be neat—giving your own mother a bridal shower!

In another letter home I told Jeanette she would have to come to Berea College, too. She would fit right in at Fireside Industries, where they made quilts and baskets and wove coverlets. She would do well in the college, too. Hadn't Grandma Smith always said Jeanette was "good in her books"? Jeanette and I agreed that Eugene probably wouldn't go to college. He and Selma Austin would get married as soon as they finished high school.

I told Jeanette about meeting a girl at Berea, Rebecca Sterling, who was from over on Beaverdam. She'd sat across from me during orientation when we took all sorts of tests—a whole week of them—and I knew I had seen her somewhere but I couldn't remember where. At first I thought maybe she was from Florida, or Georgia, or South Carolina, and I had seen her on one of those trips I'd made with George Hawkins. I was sure I had been riding a truck when I saw her, whenever or wherever it was. When I found out she was from Beaverdam I knew how it was I remembered her.

"Do you remember," I asked her, "how you used to meet the rolling store on Saturdays?"

How did I know that? she wanted to know.

I told her I had been on the rolling store with Kermit Worley once when we came around a turn and saw her standing on the limb of an apple tree.

"That was you?" she said. "You don't look the same!"

"You do," I said.

I wrote to tell Grandma Smith I'd always thought, when she warned me about "spread natters" in the pine woods, that the real word was "adder," not "natter." But I had found out in a book I had to read that the word was "natter" before it ever became "adder."

I wrote Grandma and Grandpa Wells a letter, but I didn't mention I'd found out, from a girl who'd also had a job there, that Aunt Alma had worked that past summer at Opryland, in Nashville. I figured they knew that, and since they hadn't said anything about it, it wasn't my place to mention it.

I could write home about all sorts of things, but there was so much else I couldn't say in letters: how I remembered that time over on Beaverdam so clearly I could even tell Rebecca Sterling what she'd been wearing that Saturday morning—jeans and a yellow blouse. And she'd brought butter and strawberries, and the butter had the shape of maple leaves impressed on it. There'd been a new barn in a clearing close to the apple tree Rebecca had been standing in, and I could still smell the bitter fragrance of the green lumber, could see the dazzle of the tin roof, and the glint of new nails.

I couldn't write in a letter, either, about how I dreamed one night that fall of Grandma Smith, running under a cloud of swarming bees, beating an empty pie pan with a spoon till the swarm settled, black on a drooping pine bough. I wanted to say those things, but I hadn't found a way. And I had so many questions: I wanted to know why Gerald Scott left Newfound and never came home again; why people like Junior Crumm and Wiley Woods kept trying to leave and couldn't.

Still, the more I learned about other places, the more interesting, even mysterious, my home in the mountains grew. I had lived on Newfound Creek, and now, I was discovering, Newfound Creek lived on in me, and would live in me, no matter how far away I might travel.